Penguin Books
TILLY'S FORTUNES

Helen Asher was born in Silesia (formerly part
of Germany, but now in Poland). She migrated
to Australia in the 1950s, and settled in Sydney
in 1970. *Tilly's Fortunes* is her first novel.

— TILLY'S FORTUNES —

Helen Asher

PENGUIN BOOKS

Penguin Books Australia Ltd,
487 Maroondah Highway, P.O. Box 257
Ringwood, Victoria, 3134, Australia
Penguin Books Ltd,
Harmondsworth, Middlesex, England
Penguin Books,
40 West 23rd Street, New York, N.Y. 10010, U.S.A.
Penguin Books (Canada) Limited,
2801 John Street, Markham, Ontario, Canada L3R 1B4
Penguin Books (N.Z.) Ltd,
182-190 Wairau Road, Auckland 10, New Zealand

First published by Penguin Books Australia, 1986

Typeset in 11/12 pt Palatino by Leader Composition Pty Ltd
Made and printed in Australia by Dominion Press-Hedges & Bell

Asher, Helen.
Tilly's fortunes.

ISBN 0 14 008441 X.

I. Title.

A823'.3

When I decided to get pregnant I said, if I have children, I'll have to work for the rest of my life to make the world safer for them.

Jo Vallentine
WA Senator for Nuclear Disarmament

CONTENTS

The Child   5
The Adolescent   42
The Woman   87

I stepped across the glass of brandy on the floor. My foot was heavy. The glass fell over. I walked on towards the staircase.

The child hung on to me. One of her arms had lassoed my thigh, the other was slung around my middle. Charged with emotion she pranced and trembled. By the time I had managed two steps, her limbs were woven into my skirt, her fingernails dug into me. The pain was negligible, almost sweet compared to the pain that had come like a tidal wave, only a minute ago.

She mewed, pulling my skirt. I ignored her desire to vanish from sight. Under the circumstances, the climb was endless, my sense of perspective threatened.

From the level of our apartment, it was twenty steps to the top of the building. On the landing her mewing became a lament. 'No, please, don't go.'

I stopped and enveloped her in my arms. We rocked together like we used to do when she was a baby. Soon my skirt was soaked with her tears. From the window above, the light of a young blue night fell on us.

A sudden despondency came over me, stealing my breath. I would be asked to carry the torch, to deliver compassion, to dam up the flood that had begun to ripple around our feet.

Again I looked at the window. The light was soft, and it filled me with strength. At first my voice was insubstantial, but I put my trust in it and to the best of my ability I began to talk her out of her confusion. She listened to me greedily, and while I talked about the past we passed through the present unfeeling.

'Did I ever tell you how I met your father? It happened like this. One day he came to the hotel I worked in. "I want to make some inquiries about a room," he said. "I was just passing and thought – " He stopped and stared at me.

' "Certainly," I said zealously.

' "It is not for me," he said, "it's a business arrangement."

'He wore a light grey suit and a navy blue tie crossed with a red stripe. To avoid his stare, I focused on the red stripe, but not for long. Hypnotized, we stared at each other, and I forgot where I was.

' "Yes," I said forlornly.

' "Yes," he said after me.

'It became such a nonsense that we laughed. I noticed that he was in the habit of touching a tiny mole on his upper lip. Do you remember how he always touches the mole?

'I had never seen him before yet his face was familiar, like that of a father or brother. The next day he came with the man who wanted the room. There was no need for him to accompany him, really, but it gave him an excuse to see me again.

'He held out his hand across the desk, and I came forward and put mine in his without hesitation. The other man looked on. He saw us falling in love. I didn't care. I was a changed person, happy and warm. I felt I could do anything. To your father giving love meant giving warmth. And he never lost his touch – until now.

'We must be brave, we must go up there and face him. Is he still up there?'

I shouldn't have asked. She nodded and trembled.

'He was always gentle,' I reminded her, to drug her fear and support her trust in me.

We continued to climb. I dragged her with me step after step. Questions loomed large, obstructing the way. Was this the end of my loving? Was there a law of genesis by which I functioned? By the ambiguous law of justice Carter had been expected to accept inhuman conditions, to lower himself beyond the executioners. But he hadn't.

Only three more steps. At the height of our faces the rooftop had come into view. Her arms fell away from me. Released of her dead weight I breathed easy and bent down to caress her where she clung to the second last step like a cat with her claws out.

'I'll be with you, my pet. There is nothing to be afraid of any longer, believe me.' Could I evoke a magical memory out of those devastating impressions? Poor little rabbit. 'You are safe, my pet, quite safe.'

She stayed behind when I stepped out on the rooftop. The sun was almost gone now, the dimming veil of night about to fall across the sky.

Carter stood near the parapet, quite alone. My heart contracted.

O Carter, I've lost you.

He stood like a pillar, beyond words, expelled from our hearts. I rushed forward like an avenging angel and came to a halt before his ghostly appearance. The decision had to be made calmly.

I turned around. At the entrance Ella was peeping around the corner, her eyes popping. She was on her hands and knees.

I went over to Carter and positioned myself close

to him. He didn't look at me, but his head tilted with the weight of his conscience. I raised my arm. My hands opened and closed, undecided what to do.

The child looked on, waiting for the world to come together again. My hands descended on Carter's head, which was ready to receive the blow that would split it in two.

But fate melted us together once more, the statuesque couple, arms wound around each other's shoulders and heads sunk from their stems in grief's dark folds.

After a time of insurmountable sadness, there was a stir inside. It was a wish for regression.

THE CHILD

A midwife drew me from my mother, pressing her hard fingers into my soft skull. As a result, I was branded with dimples in my temples, and I can't be convinced otherwise.

With a sigh of relief, and a flourishing smile, she was about to let me hang upside down, when I opened my eyes to the light of a copper-tinged world, and it was then that the midwife noticed me wholly. Her mouth split open to a deep silly hole, and half in awareness of my tenderness, half abrupt, she dropped me back between my mother's legs, forgetting to smack my red crumpled bottom.

'Oooouuuuh,' she yelped like a wolf. 'Oooouuuuh.'

'Good grief, O deary me,' she stammered, so that my exhausted mother imagined that something was wrong with me, that I had entered the world with no arms or four, or eight nipples – if I was a girl – or as a Siamese twin or a hermaphrodite.

Restful for the moment, I lay in the bloodsmell around me, befriending myself with a brand new world, which, to begin with, was colder and larger than the one I had lived in before. I stretched my arms and legs and, since there was nothing to stop me, I stirred and straddled freely to give vent to my wonderful energy. Changes occurred in rapid succession, as if I was touched by magic. Notions of possibilities moved me, and expectations sank in my heart like a windblown seed, but my newly born rapture came to a halt when a thunderous voice turned me as stiff as a poker.

'What's the matter?' my mother cried out. 'I want to know, no matter what. Lift it up, show it to me!'

The midwife, a woman of an agitated disposition, was quiet at once. Recollections of her sins tumbled through my mother's head.

The midwife obeyed automatically and lifted me up so that now I was face to face with my mother. But one of us was upside down, and feeling weird. I cried for help.

'Good God,' my mother whispered, turning pale with shock, 'a hydrocephalus.'

'No, it's not that,' the midwife said in a falsetto voice, turning me around so that I was in a more comfortable position.

I snapped my breath. The manipulation had made me dizzy.

'She just has a very high forehead. It'll come good; she'll grow out of it. Once her hair has grown, it won't be so noticeable. It's her eyes that are – remarkable – don't you see, her huge golden eyes, the size of saucers.'

'Not that big,' my mother said in my defence, putting her bewildered head back on the pillow.

'And golden,' the midwife said.

'More yellow, I'd say,' my mother said.

There was a solemn pause.

'She's beautiful,' the midwife said dutifully.

The false tone in the woman's voice saddened my mother. 'Ugly, I'd say, with that long oval head,' she answered with painful honesty. Like the midwife, she was conditioned to find slit eyes and round skulls beautiful. 'She reminds me of – ' But she couldn't establish the resemblance.

'Yes,' the midwife agreed,' she reminds me of something too – of someone, I mean.'

Interesting noises began to fill the air, tinkering, swishing and the midwife's lilting. I had come out of the turmoil unharmed and was in harmony with the midwife's song when she lifted me up and dipped me into a warm cosy liquid. I moved my arms with delight. Where was I now? Had I returned to the pool of life? Was I a pearl in a shell or a speck of gold in a ripple of water? Or was I of a higher order?

I signalled my contentment.

'Ah,' the midwife said in her friendliest manner, 'isn't that nice? You like that, don't you?'

• 2 •

Alone with my mother I cried to her. The house is so big I am lost in it. And what is the meaning of this? As soon as I move my arms, something cold touches me. I must tell you how I loathe hanging in the air, how it terrifies me. Please never let me hang upside down again.

I want to be close to you again. Please, let me back in. I don't know where I am and why I am here. O, things have changed so much. When I was inside you, a disturbance was like a dream. It woke me up but never threatened my life. Once your voice was soft, not cutting like it is now. I remember when you slipped and fell. Thump I went, and my heart went flying. Another time I heard a woman shout at you. You were shaken with anger and humiliation, so that I too was shaken. I've got to tell you many things. I want you to listen. Listen –'

'Hush,' my mother interjected.

I wanted her to pay attention to my dilemma, but most of all I wanted to reclaim my natural place. I cried even louder. She cut me off, and I screamed.

My mother, from an unfathomable distance, tried to appease me until an unbearable sob throttled me and I kept quiet not to be gagged again.

A neighbour came with a bottle of brown malt beer for my mother's recuperation. 'To build up your blood again,' she said, handing it over.

'It's kind of you,' said my mother. To draw attention to me she rocked my basket. It woke me up.

'You have a beautiful child,' the neighbour said without conviction. 'Where did she get her golden eyes?'

'From God,' my mother said plainly. She fell silent and plucked her quilt.

'O yes?' said the woman with a voice as thin as a razorblade.

I stared at her with my big golden eyes until she stirred on her chair, jumped to her feet, mumbled an excuse and left.

My mother was quiet for a long time. She let her

hand slip into my basket but much too soon she removed it again and placed it on her chest.

A downy silence settled around us. A desire had welled up inside me, however, and I began to stir. My mother didn't take any notice of it. She was in a world of her own. Agitated, I kicked the cover. Sounds formed in my mouth, but they didn't come out. As I was fumbling, my thumb came across my mouth, and I docked it there and went to sleep like a flower.

• 3 •

My mother was poor. She lived in a room that contained only the necessary furniture and a wooden box covered with household paper. From a distance it had the appearance of cloth because of the printed flowers on it. It was large and she called it the Wonder-what's-in-it box.

The window was draped with a copper-tone curtain that originally fitted a larger window. It fell down in deep pocket-like folds. My mother would have loved long lacy curtains, the sort that look like a bridal veil, and a red velvet box to make the Wonder-what's-in-it box look like a treasure chest. She would also have liked to own a rocking chair and a cosy table lamp with a white or pink lampshade.

There is a saying among poor people that Job wasn't the poorest man on earth for he still had a goat. My mother said she was poorer than Job because a goat was a source of free milk. But once she said, 'If you don't have anything, not even a goat, you mustn't think that you've missed out on blessings. I was given a voice to sing. It pleases me and makes me happy.'

I don't know whether she had a great voice, but it was strong and convincing. She was transformed when she sang, looking as beautiful as a lilac bush or a crystal. She detached herself from her surroundings, a fixed expression in her eyes, her head held rigid and her chest expanding. She was an impressive sight. Her songs were a private pleasure, but sometimes she took them further, to please someone up on high.

On a summer evening she would often sing when she left the curtain open to save electricity by not turning on the light. Waiting for the moon to come around and squeeze between the two houses, she would sing, turning her face towards the moon when it arrived. Or she would sing in the late afternoon standing at the table cutting vegetables for our meal. Something must have touched her and ordered her to sing, and while she slowly scraped the carrots or cut the cabbage she poured out her song.

I liked her to sing hunting songs or the song of the child who had lost his father who was killed in a big fire.

When I knew the words, I tried to sing like my mother. I placed myself beside her, stepping on a footstool, looking at the moon and cutting softly into a vegetable. My voice was small, scratchy and without bounce. I pressed my chest out, bending my head back to emphasize my conviction, but I couldn't sing like my mother, who didn't emphasize anything at all.

My mother said, 'You have your eyes to be glad

about.'

But they didn't engender that lovely feeling a voice does.

My father was unknown to me. He didn't have huge golden eyes, my mother once said. She was right then to tell the neighbour that I had them from God. My father didn't seem to have been a likable man.

One day my mother said, 'I'm a humble servant. A humble servant doesn't ask for much. She hopes for good working conditions and decent treatment. When I worked for your father, I hoped to be treated with respect. Respect means a lot in a servant's position. It means as much as money. Or more.'

I didn't understand her position then, though I felt there was pain in her heart.

My father had no shape in my head. I prefer to think that he is dead.

• 4 •

My mother gave birth to me without happiness in her heart. Though poverty and disillusion were her lot, she had the strength of simplicity on her side and stood up to affliction without complaining.

I remember my mother's lap in which I nestled when we sat in front of the fire. Her clothes smelled of potatoes roasted in an open fire or of the smoke of pine wood, and she allowed me to play with her hands, which were always rough and stained from the dark soil.

Watching the flames and leaning towards the warmth, her spirits rose. Magic mingled with her modest contentment. Behind us the walls of the half-dark room flashed with the reflections of the quivering flames.

She sang a song for me. Usually it was the song of the prince and the princess who couldn't get together because of a vicious interfering old nun. The prince had to cross a lake to get to the princess. It was agreed that she put a light in the window for his direction, but the nun removed the light, and the prince was lost in the dark sea.

'Your eyes are so deep and golden – like two cups of liquid gold,' my mother said to me one evening in front of the fire. I thought of God who had given me my eyes, but not for long.

My presence compensated for her loneliness, but my mother never spoke intimately or imaginatively to me. Perhaps there were men in her life who meant something to her. I don't know. To me all men were uncles.

This she said about her parents. 'My father once hit my mother. He hit her!' She shouted with hurt and flung her arm in front of her face. Then it dropped and hung at her side as if it were paralysed. I sat there with my mouth open and swallowed air.

'Where is my grandmother?' I wanted to know when I learned that relatives share our blood and often share our house and lives.

'Your grandmother,' she said, 'had a stone inside her that grew and grew, and when it had no more room to grow she twisted her head ninety degrees and died.'

'Oh,' I said, with a respectful fear of stones. I never spoke of my grandmother to anyone.

Most of her thoughts my mother kept to herself. I

didn't know her feelings like I knew mine, which spread out like red inkspots on a sheet of blotting paper.

My hair grew long and yellow. I was a flaxen-head, or a lightning-head as my mother called me sometimes in front of others. I especially liked to be called lightning-head.

When we walked along the street, my hand holding the hem of her skirt, people turned their heads and bleated: 'Oooouuuuh.'

Or they gloated and whispered, 'She reminds me of – '

I wonder of whom I reminded them.

My mother often said, 'Do this – ' or, 'Don't do that,' and I grew hesitant and stopped doing anything. Instead I sulked.

She always carried a handkerchief in her sleeve or pocket, which she wet with her saliva to wipe my mouth. I struggled against her, twisting my head and body like a captured worm to escape, but she anticipated my reaction, held me in a clamp between her thighs and didn't let go of me until my mouth was clean.

The smell of her saliva was repulsive, a concentrate of intimacy. When she had finished, I stood back half a step, spat into her skirt and wiped my mouth with my own saliva.

My mother told me not to eat the mucous I poked out of my nose, which I had never thought of doing anyhow. She knew a little girl who ate her mucous. She hated it and thought that I might get into the habit too. But I had my own method of disposing of it. Depending where I was, I deposited the tiny balls under the soles of my shoes, or under a tabletop, or on a house wall. I liked to keep my handkerchief clean for special purposes.

• 5 •

We moved to the land of Abundance where the earth is carpeted green and the animals are as important as human beings. It is the land of milk, fruit and honey. But I didn't like honey. I liked jam, and I could have as much jam as I wanted. And sausages, and yeast cakes. My mother sometimes bought buns that were plaited like the hair of blonde peasant girls. My favourite buns were those that were smothered with icing sugar.

The poor room faded out of my dim occult world. I knew about it from my mother's descriptions, which moored in my existence like some fairytale, evoking the impression that my consciousness was clear from the beginning.

In this rich country I met an old woman. She sat in a plush chair sewing flowers into a dress of white voile, and I stood beside her and watched the flower garland grow around the hem and the sleeves, which opened out like butterfly wings. It was the most beautiful dress I had ever seen.

The old woman nodded and smiled when I told her.

'I never had one like it myself,' she said, gently stroking the voile with her old freckled hands. I felt sorry for her.

One morning the dress hung over our chair and my mother said, 'It's yours.'

I slipped into it and ran outside. As I swayed

14

through the meadows my heart was light in my chest.

My ear captured a voice, 'She reminds me of – '

'An angel,' I rejoiced and ran uphill.

On top was a wooden tower. Above the tower a bunch of creamy clouds were scrambled together. Before I came to the top, I stopped in my tracks. I shook my head. It was funny, but I couldn't go all the way to the tower, and I didn't know why. The hill blocked the view to the other side, but I knew in my heart that when you went past the tower unlimited adventure would begin. One day I would make the grade. It would take time. I had to grow tall and courageous.

Country life was fine. There I had a cousin, and together we ventured into forbidden gardens and discovered new meadows and unending forests. Sometimes we were carried away by the games we played. We galloped alongside a field like horses, flew like screeching geese through silent laneways, changed into lions, and when it took our fancy transformed ourselves into mother and father.

Once we went to an apple orchard. The next house was out of sight, so far away that it almost didn't exist. The sun was shining, making gold and gemstones which in a million years would be dug out of the ground. We dived into the high grass. I lay on my back trying to look into the sky where I knew angels were sitting on white clouds, like the paper angels my mother had bought me. They're the ones who lean their chin into the palm of their hands and look thoughtfully into the distance. Do they see anything? Do they see God? My cousin said no, but my mother said yes.

In the apple orchard, my cousin's face got in the way, blocking my view of the sky so that I was forced to look into his blue watery eyes. He smelled of mud and the juices of grass, but his clothes smelled of the dried pears and prunes that his mother prepared and kept in large bags under the family's beds.

In the apple orchard my cousin wriggled about. He ripped out a seeded spear of grass and tickled my face with it. I sneezed and spluttered. He wriggled closer to me, and the closeness between us was different from the closeness between my mother and me, but I couldn't define the difference. My cousin showed me where my body's centre of well-being was, and when he pressed it with his finger I felt the trees and flowers spring.

· 6 ·

One night in my dream I had been flying through the air and had fallen from a height into a forest among wild boars. To save myself from being savaged, my defence mechanism was alerted, and I woke up.

I was surrounded by an impenetrable darkness. When I called out for my mother, there was no answer. She wasn't there. I pricked up my ears. The darkness intensified. I trembled like an aspen leaf.

I was caught inside something that had no outside, and everything I knew was caught in it too. My bed was submerged in darkness like a ship that had sunk to the bottom of the sea.

Despairing, I left my bed and started walking, my arms extended, but I had lost my sense of direction. There was the door. No. It was a wall. I hit my head and whimpered, bit my lip not to draw the attention of ghosts and demons. Was that the window? No. I hit my shin. Tears came to my eyes. I touched wood, brick and cloth, but hands need intelligent guidance to be of any help.

By chance I found the window, and finally my eyes fastened on a light. It disappeared, popping up somewhere else. Gone again. But I knew what it was. It was the beautiful but insidious light of the swamp. Yes, I knew about people who had walked into the moor and been swallowed up by it.

I dropped to the floor and from there I saw a skyful of stars. They were ominous and strange. No communication was possible, no connection between them and me. They were the warder to the inside that had no outside. Gazing at them made me numb.

The night played tricks on me. Where was my bed? My arms paddled in front of me, pushing aside wall after wall, palpable and impalpable ones.

I hit my chin again, but I had found my bed. Trembling, I touched the warmth the sheets had retained. My eyes needed no force to close. My mother was gone. I was a prisoner of the night. I hid under the cover, looking for comfort. I clung to my thumb, and I sucked it hard.

I am Tilly, I said to myself. I am lightning-head. I am not afraid of the dark. I know mysteries, about the tower on top of the hill and the swamp that devours people. I am Tilly. I am important. As important as our creek.

• 7 •

The comely hill was surrounded by a forest that

grew mushrooms and berries of a tempting sweet-ness. I penetrated the bushes, grasped and gulped and smacked my lips. I was insatiable. The sun climbed up and down. My neck began to hurt.

Half way up the hill lived my uncle, the tailor. He sat on top of his table, his legs crossed.

'Did you come for remnants, Tilly?' he asked.

I nodded.

He gave me a dull remnant and a bright one. My heart thumped for the bright one. It was one for girls. I would safe-keep it in my treasure box with the marbles and the paper angels and play with it occasionally.

The comely hill was an easy one, not as high as the hill with the wooden tower, and it had a church that was reached by a winding path. But I avoided the church, which was so big and daunting.

Sometimes, instead of going straight to my uncle's house, I would walk to the forest for berries or mushrooms, or just to find out what was going on in the bushes. Sometimes, out of the tangle of trees came a deer. Seeing me it would stand still, and we would stare at each other. In that moment I would hear the forest whisper, and everything was respectful.

One day, after I had been to the forest, I went to my uncle's house to ask for some more remnants. At the side of the house where I seldom passed, there on the ground tiny flowers peeped out between the green. The leaves were large, and the flowers looked shy.

Lying flat on my belly, I looked at them closely and separated the green from the wonderful colours I had never seen before.

I picked one of the little things to try and eat it as I sometimes do with leaves or grasses, but found I couldn't. Into my nostrils streamed a bewitching scent. In an instant I dipped my face into the bunch on the ground, inhaling slowly, exhaling quickly.

Just as I had with the berries, I grew greedy again. Thoughtlessly, I began to savage the patch when a voice from above said sternly, 'Tilly, what are you doing?'

It was a woman's voice and belonged to my aunt whose hair is wavy and who wears seductive colours.

'You're picking all my violets,' she scolded me. 'Stop that, will you!'

'Violets,' I breathed and devoured the name as I wished to do with the flowers. 'I want them,' I said pertly.

'You can keep those you've already taken, but promise not to take more.'

'Promise!' I was already on my flight down the hill, home to my mother.

When I arrived I cried, 'Smell them, mother, smell them,' and when she leaned over, I pushed them in her face.

She did as I had done. She inhaled slowly and exhaled quickly and uttered moans of delight in which I recognized an ache that is joy for the miracle in her tailor brother's garden.

• 8 •

'Old man,' I said, 'can I see your rabbits?'

'He isn't old,' said my mother, embarrassed.

———

I taxed him freely. 'But he's a giant,' I said, 'and he has two deep wrinkles between his eyes. He must be old.'

'He's young,' my mother insisted, pulling my hair, turning red and shuffling her feet, while the controversial man looked down on me, astonished and kind of silly. His eyes were not as deep as my mother's but as shallow as our creek, which only reaches up to my knees at its deepest.

'O yes,' I agreed, because that was what my mother wanted, and I smiled to make her happy and him sympathetic towards my demand. 'Can I see your rabbits now?'

'Yes,' he said and walked ahead of us. His long legs, wrapped in corduroy, were at my eye level. By the creases above, you could tell that he didn't have much of a bottom.

The rabbits lived in small cages, five or six in one cage. Their fur was spotted as if a painter had smudged a brush on them, and when I poked my finger through the mesh wire, their skin twitched.

'I want a rabbit,' I said.

'No,' said my mother.

'Yes,' I said, 'I want a rabbit to take to bed.'

'Rabbits can only live in cages,' the giant said, looking serious.

'No,' I said, 'I don't believe it. You haven't thought about it properly. I know you can hold them and cuddle them.'

My gentle wish was not granted, and I went down to the swamp around the lake where the water lilies grow, surrounding it in a wreath. I tried to reach them, my weight balanced on the toes of one foot, my arm stretched out far, and the other leg swinging away from me.

I couldn't reach them. I couldn't possess them either.

I sat down in the grass and watched them. Their bright golden faces nodded tentatively. I could have watched them forever.

There was no sound. Life when it calls has no voice. But I jumped on my legs and ran away as if I had been called by my name.

· 9 ·

We moved to the city again. I don't know why. But I like to think that my mother had some higher aim. People in the country are fresh faced, simple and sure about their place in the world. The cradle of their mind is a soft green meadow. I suppose that is a good way to be.

Country people, who often smell heartily of clover and camomile, are made in haystacks and potato fields. I know this because my cousin, who smells of dried pears and prunes, whispered it into my ear. I suppose it is good to be made in haystacks.

What could my mother have aimed for? For laced curtains? For a special man? Perhaps she liked the lifts and elevators as I do and went to the city so she could be thrilled by the height at the top of the buildings.

I knew very little about my mother. I never asked her to tell me about herself, and she never asked me about myself. We talked together as a way of passing information.

We still had our likes for jam and sausages, of

which we ate plenty. But not all the time. If my mother asked me what I wanted to eat, I always said barley soup.

'Not again,' she'd say and after that she wouldn't ask me for a while.

We lived in a house that left its mark on me. I remember the bare greyish walls that surrounded my bed, like prison walls. My bed, which was as big as my mother's, was as comfortable as can be. I loved it as much as I hated the house that was owned by a witch with black piercing eyes. As soon as she caught sight of me she stopped and stared. Did she bewitch other people too? If only I knew.

It was part of the spell that I couldn't talk about it. I couldn't ask my mother how she felt about the witch I thought was freezing my tongue. She was so powerful and vicious if she wanted to be. Her shadow followed me around. If I opened my mouth to tell on her, she would seek revenge, coming in the night to drink my blood and inject my dreams with a horrifying madness.

In order to leave the house, I had to overcome the distance between our rooms in the back of the house to the foregarden. We didn't have separate entrances. With my neck drawn, I swished through the gloomy corridor as if pursued by the devil, past a mirror that showed a distorted face. Was that me? At the door I took a deep breath. I stretched and welcomed the day outside. With a few jumps, I reached the gate. The moment I stood on the other side, her power had ceased.

Inside the house, she was able to see me everywhere. The walls were no protection. The mirror was proof to me that I was under her spell. Every time I passed I was forced to turn my head, to face my own fear.

She haunted me day and night. I could not move freely and spoke and breathed with restriction. At night, to enforce my defences, I ended my prayer with several amens.

What puzzled me was that in her front garden sweet peas and wall flowers grew in profusion.

• 10 •

In spring a big cockroach came flying into our room. I picked it up and put it in a matchbox, and maintained it with a leaf on which it could nibble and sleep at the same time. The bug refused to eat the leaf.

When it is really hungry it will eat it, I thought, because everyone eats when they are really hungry. Leaves are his favourite food, and he will not go on striking for long if he wants to survive.

I wasn't fond of cockroaches. They are coarse and repulsive to touch and make my skin prickle. But I was its master of life and death! This outweighed my aversion.

Two days later I found a better home for my inferior, a green round tin with a mirror inside, which I was willing to leave at his disposal so that he could lead a more luxurious life.

The tin smelled enchanting. I had exchanged it for my bead purse, because I loved the smell better than my purse, although I liked the purse very much and wouldn't have exchanged it for anything else. No, that isn't quite the truth. I could be tempted to exchange it for the picture of a beautiful woman on thick shiny paper. Her name was Greta Garbo.

'You must be joking,' my friend Jola said to me. 'Your silly purse in exchange for Queen Christine?'

'I thought you said her name was Greta Garbo,' I said.

'She was also Queen Christine,' Jola said. 'She is both, see. My mother said so.'

It troubled me that this queen was worth so much I couldn't afford her picture. Some things you can want really desperately.

It was my mother who said the scribble on the tin was 4711. I asked her if there were other good smelling numbers.

'No,' she said.

To my regret the cockroach by the name of Philip lived only for a few hours in his nice smelling house. Then he died.

• 11 •

After we left the bewitched house we lived in several others in which there was no sign of witchcraft. Still when I think about it my blood curdles. But I must say this, while I called the woman a witch, my mother's opinion of her was that she was cracked. It did not influence my impression of her. Meanwhile I grew and almost reached my mother's height. She had to make new dresses for me and told me, 'Next year you probably can wear mine.'

I was pleased about being tall but not about being skinny.

One day we moved into a house that was owned by tall slow-moving people. They were taller than anyone I knew, looking down on everyone standing near them. Height, it seemed to me, equals power, but these people looked sleepy and unaware of their power. They rose in the morning at the rooster's first crow.

The rooster was beautifully curved and clothed in shimmering feathers. He stalked through the garden like a king, and I loved him. I wished I could maintain such a posture. He often stood on the chopping block in the backyard, which was partly planted with vegetables.

A few days later I saw him. Even later when I knew his name I ignored it. He was standing right behind our door when I went out, the son of the tall slow-moving people, himself very tall and large-limbed.

When he saw me, he sang out, 'One-two-three' and did some push-ups and threw his limbs about in a foolish manner. I blushed at his antics.

Of course, I knew what he was getting at. He had been peeping through the keyhole, watching me do my exercises.

The 'exercises' were a secret. I never did them in front of my mother, and I was angry that he had unmasked me.

In the beginning the exercises had been genuine, but one day I had caught sight of myself in the wardrobe mirror. I stared at myself, and when I recovered I continued with my exercises, only now my movements were less rigid. They flowed nicely, and I thought maybe I would become a dancer. Soon it was a certainty.

The tall boy had no regard for the finer things. He

was crude and unsophisticated, and he didn't let go of me. With stilted legs, I walked up the street. He followed me. It looked as if we were invisibly connected, as if we had something in common. But that wasn't all. From the distance he pelted me with offensive words. Words from the gutter. I would never use such words.

I sat down in the park up the road to read the book Jola lent me. She was two years older and had already grown breasts, but they were still very small. Since she had started to swell up there, she had taken to giggling and affected behaviour.

Jola said I must read this book, and the most important passages she had marked. I could skip the rest. That was boring, she said.

The boy loitered about for a while and suddenly ran away. Not much later he came back on his bicycle, riding round the tree, the bench and me, sometimes just missing my toes. I moved my lips without a sound, looking at him as if he were beyond comprehension, until I remembered that I don't have eyes like other people, and I looked into my book. After a while he gave up and with mad noises raced down the street, leaving me to read in peace.

Reading is fun. I look at people – the teachers, for instance, or him – and I wonder who they are, what are their secrets? In books people reveal their secrets and unfold from mysteries, and some are funny. People you meet are mainly physical; they have little to give you. They indulge in small talk, and I get the impression that half the time they don't mean what they say. Characters in books are good and bad at the same time, wise and dumb, thinking and unthinking. People you talk to complain about others and put themselves on a pedestal.

My mother is an exception. She listens attentively and is modest, and she looks like a madonna with her fine smile and the tilt of her head. I would like to ask her what she thinks, but I know she can't tell me. She can't describe her feelings.

When he realized how much I admired the rooster, he chased him around the yard to upset me, and one day the rooster lay dead on the chopping block. That was his doing, for certain.

Never before had I made anyone feel bad, but now I didn't care. I waited for a long time beside the chopping block for him to show up, mourning the rooster and touching his beautiful feathers for the first time. I am touching death, I thought with a shiver, but when the shiver was gone I felt that death was not monstrous but still and featherlight.

He came around the corner to face me. I took a deep angry breath. 'I'll never forgive you for killing the rooster,' I yelled. 'I'll never talk to you again in all my life, I swear it.' And I spat on the ground to show him what he was worth.

'He's dead, he's dead,' he laughed and stomped his hooves like a bull.

Was he insane? I stood like a pillar just looking at him. He couldn't bear it and squirmed.

'He isn't worth anything. He's good for the pot, that's all,' he shouted.

'He was beautiful,' I said coldly, 'which is more than I can say for you. You look like a giraffe. He was defenceless and innocent and desirable. You are repulsive.'

He lifted the rooster and holding it in front of him he came towards me. I ran inside and locked the door.

From that day on silence separated us, icy cold and hostile. I think he understood that when I stared at him I was saying that the death of the rooster would be on his conscience forever. I would not let him forget it.

The following winter he came down with the flu.

'She hates me,' he said when he was wrung out with fever.

'Who hates you?' his mother asked.

'Tilly,' he whispered. 'She thinks she's a dancer.'

He had given away my secret.

The minute I knew he was dead my attitude to him changed. I thought of him often and felt sorry for him because he died so young. I felt sorry for his clumsiness and his long wobbly neck. I imagined that he had suffered from my coldness. The rooster was demoted, but with a reservation.

'He wasn't a happy boy,' my mother said. 'He didn't have any friends. He walked down the street talking to himself.'

I went to see Jola.

'What's that?' she said poking at my doll.

'What does it look like?'

'Dolls are for kids.' She turned away. She thought she was smart.

'You're stupid,' I said. That would set her straight. I was right.

'Stay,' she said when I walked out of the door.

'No, I'm in mourning.'

'Who died?'

'He died.'

But you weren't in love with him. Why mourn him?'

'Because it's decent.'

I went home, because the doll was an embarrassment. I propped her up on my bed, took her down again and chucked her in the wardrobe.

Was I still a kid or what? The question went up in smoke. I ran out into the street looking for someone who'd go with me to the park or the shopping centre. But I had to go on my own. There wasn't anyone around – unless the ghost at my heels was not imagined.

• 12 •

Bacchus is so divine with the grapes in his hair and his round soft belly and his voluptuous lips. Your hands, my beloved, are a little too padded, and your toes are a little too knobbly, but I will close my eyes to your faults, my love; they are minor, nothing, really. But how would I like to stroke your adorable chest, sing in praise of the curves of your shoulders and kiss the taste of wine from your lips.

I can't have him. Someone has taken his penis from him. I wonder who knocked it off. Who could be so cruel, so uncouth and impudent? What use is a penisless lover.

But I can love you with my soul, my adorable one. Yes, my soul will love you forever.

I adorn my wall with pictures of David, Adam, Brutus, Victor, Guilliano and Lorenzo de Medici, and I can never make up my mind which one I prefer. Until I come to rest with him, the man above all the august men. Jesus, so endearing and tender, so venerable and yet so tempting.

Love is in my head, and love is in my heart.

'You are dreaming again,' my mother said, finding me starry eyed.

'I am not,' I said. 'I'm wide awake. They're real. You'll never go to Florence to see them. I will. I know I will.'

'What are you talking about?' my mother said, and I know she was blaming everything on my eyes.

'About David and Brutus,' I answered.

'Oh, Brutus,' she said. 'He was evil.'

'Why was he evil?' I asked.

'I don't know. They say he was evil.'

'I love him,' I said.

'You silly thing,' she said. 'He's dead and gone.'

'Not gone,' I said. 'It doesn't matter if he is not in the flesh. And I love Michelangelo. Will I grow breasts like La Notte?'

'Who is La Notte?' she asked.

'The Woman of the Night,' I said.

'Don't worry about your breasts,' she said, looking at me with the darkened eyes of worry. 'Why don't you get busy with something else? And if it has to be fancy people or dead idols, why don't you take an interest in Charlie Chaplin?'

'Phew, Charlie Chaplin,' I said. 'No, I prefer Brutus. Brutus! Taste his name on your tongue. B R U T U S! It sounds strong and invincible. And I do worry about my breasts. I would resent having breasts like La Notte.'

'What breasts has she got?' my mother asked, shyly, shamefully.

'Here, see for yourself,' I said and showed her La Notte's breasts in my book.

She shook her head, and her eyes sank to the floor.

'I always thought you were different,' she said. 'My eyes don't see things the way yours do.'

'My eyes are like everyone else's,' I said. 'They are! They are!'

'All right,' she said to calm me.

I went into our bedroom. I sat down on my mother's bed opposite mine to look at Bacchus, Brutus and the others on the wall beside my bed.

Finally the warm old colours filled with life, a door unlocked before me, the scene opened up and I moved inside, until I was there, at the conversion of St Paul.

• 13 •

I paint my little breasts red, my mouth to look like a rose. A string of beads dangles from my narrow hips, cascading between my things. The dance is on. My breasts bob and swing and tremble like jelly. I'm a woman, a woman.

Forces combine like thunder in the sky. The walls echo and tremble, the air is vibrating. Music splashes around me and rushes forth, spreading like the embracing waters. My arms float on a note, my body bends willingly under the baton. Hallelujah, I'm a woman!'

Illustrious pictures are called for. There. Flags flutter on bridges moved by the flamboyant wind. Antelopes gallop through the veldt towards their drinking places. The sky in the west is burning. O breathless beauty! O wonderful world! Glory hallelujah!

Blossoms are lit with the light of the sun, lanterns in gardens. High in the sky the angels gather in gold-drenched ballrooms. Willingly bending under the baton.

My sweat smells of lilac. I rubbed blossoms into my skin that I stole from a neighbour's garden. Before I bruised them, I smothered them with sweet kisses. Lilac, you died for me.

Illustrious pictures are called for. Tan-tan-tara! Golden trumpets blow jubilation to the heavens. Russia is about to be conquered, and later it will be the world. Blow, trumpet, blow!

Life is love. My love is perfect. Tan-tan-tara! Tilly Flaxen-head today is a woman. Come out, secret, don't be a coward.

The '1812 Overture' is dust and dead. Napoleon is dead. The air is listless. My body is damp. But I am strong, very strong. This body is ready and willing.

What are you saying?

Mary, holy mother, protect me from myself because I'm prepared to be unholy.

Be ashamed of yourself, she says.

Who says?

Let go of me, warder of my conscience, look at me! I am standing proud.

The beads nudge my thigh. My thighs are wet. Blood is coming from inside me, accompanied by a little pain. Everywhere in my body pulses throb. Barriers are overthrown. Fuses blown.

'What are you doing?' my mother said from the doorway.

'I was dancing.'

'Wash off the paint,' my mother said from the doorway, turning into an icicle. Her mouth, encrusted with bitterness, withered before my eyes.

I went to wash off the paint, from my breasts, my mouth. I sat down on the floor as if I had been caned and beaten.

My mother said no more. Absentminded or strangely divided, she sat there with heavy shoulders, a big old mamma, fumbling with my string of beads, which in her hands turned into a rosary.

It was so sad. The rosary, the '1812 Overture', lilac and all. We were sad and sorry for what should be so joyous.

• 14 •

I don't remember my mother's kisses. She was probably too shy to kiss anyone, whether for love, friendship or simply for joy. When she touched me, it was for practical reasons. As a matter of routine, she bathed me and washed my hair. She cut my toenails and manicured my fingernails until I began to grow breasts. Her touch was firm and pleasant.

I don't remember my mother's breasts. She must have disguised them so as not to draw attention to them.

I don't remember her patting me or tickling me gently to show her affection. She was unaware of the love link between people, ignorant of endorsing the fact of love.

Once I saw her crying. It was such a depressing sight.

'Mamma,' I said. 'I know a terrific joke. Listen.'

She listened, still sobbing, but afterwards she didn't cry anymore, and I was pleased.

I never saw my mother in a red, orange, purple or yellow dress. I suspect she feared the reflection of unrelenting colours on her image.

She handled her undergarments in the most clandestine way. White, the most sensitive colour, was the colour to wear next to the skin. Secretly, though it was no secret to me, she was in love with innocence. Since she had lost hers, she had mine at heart.

'Don't let strange men touch you,' she said, with a shifting look.

Perhaps once a year we took the topaz brooch out of its case and put it back when we had admired it for a while. She had inherited it from her mother who had never worn it. My mother never wore it either. She said there was never an occasion for it. I thought it must be precious and I would wear it on Sundays when one day it would be mine.

My mother had nightmares. When she uttered a cry in the middle of the night, I got out of my bed to shake her and break the spell. She said that a big dog or a similar beast had sat on her chest and wouldn't let go of her.

Sometimes my mother said cheerful things like, 'Tahiti must be a beautiful place.' But she also said, 'What would I do with a diamond? I couldn't do anything with it. I would shame the diamond.' Or, 'I don't need a new coat. I can reverse the old one, and it will look new again.'

My mother had no ambition or extraordinary desire. I think desire dies in factories. She said to me,

'Tilly, don't become a servant to a private person. Seek work in a factory when the time comes. There you serve a machine, and what you help to produce serves the whole community.'

I shook my head, ignoring the wisdom of her experience. 'I'll discover a serum to cure cancer,' I said 'or if anything, I'll be the boss of a factory.'

'How?' she said and pursed her lips.

'Because I want to,' I said.

'You will have to start off as a simple worker,' she said.

'No, not me,' I said.

'Yes,' she said. 'Life is no high-flying business.'

'It can be,' I said. 'There are high-flying people.'

I remember her sewing dresses at home, hundreds of them in a week. She sat hunchbacked with her reading glasses set far down on her nose. She showed me the money she got for her work – little money for dresses that would be very expensive in the shops.

'A small amount of money shouldn't make a person blind and sore,' she said. 'It shouldn't bend your back and give you a pain in the neck. It shouldn't, but it does. With big money, it is just the opposite. It soothes. Money is the most supercilious thing. Do you know what I mean?'

• 15 •

Something was wrong with my mother's throat, and she was admitted to a hospital. I went to see her, with a bunch of carnations and a quarter pound of chocolates. Her smile was welcoming, and I imagined what she would look like if she were wealthy

---

and spoiled. Most probably she would look beautiful and be game to wear red and yellow dresses. She would set her eyes on diamonds and find them worthy of her.

'You have the chocolates, flaxen-head,' she said with her scratchy voice. 'I know you meant well, but I can't eat them.'

'Thank you,' I said, and began to eat them.

'It is important to be beautiful,' I said, continuing my previous thought.

'You, with your funny remarks,' she said, fighting her failing voice. 'You always say what pops into your head.'

I had come to an age where I liked to mull over witty remarks, that is true. With witty remarks I almost outwitted my undesirable age.

'There are things you can do to help you to become beautiful.' I continued to lecture her. 'Like eating chocolate – yeah – or falling in love with David and Brutus. Or reading a deep, clever book, or wearing a smashing new dress.'

I spoke with my mouth full of chocolate. 'And I tell you what you should do, my little Mamma. You should wear a purple dress.'

'Purple. My goodness!' she said, 'that's too much.'

'Let's start with a purple blouse then,' I said. 'I'll buy you one as soon as I've got the money together.'

She shook her head. She would shake her head to most things that were good for her.

When I came to visit her again, her bed was empty. Perhaps she was in the operating theatre. I wondered if I should leave the oranges on her bed but decided not to. I went to look for the matron to ask her where my mother was.

Matron asked me to take a seat and took a seat herself. She folded her hands on top of the desk. Her thumbs bounced against each other. She focused on my forehead. The words, straight and black and large, flowed from her as if onto a poster.

'Your mother has just passed away. She had cancer.'

The skin of her face was like that of rice paper lanterns.

'No,' I said and heard the echo of my voice in the distance, bouncing back to me, piercing and penetrating inaccessible corners.

'No!' I shouted, fighting cyclones and the whole array of ravaging elements that had turned loose.

'No.' I shook my head and couldn't stop. 'I don't believe you. Cancerous people don't die just like that. Not so easily, not so quickly.'

'Sometimes they do.'

Voices of a high inexorable tribunal joined with her, their tongues lashing out at me.

'No,' I said. 'You gave her the wrong treatment. You neglected her. You have no feelings.'

'Child,' they said with cotton-wool voices, pawing me like a kitten.

'I am fourteen, almost fifteen, don't call me child,' I said.

When they let me say goodbye to her in the niche behind the curtain, I said goodbye to her a hundred thousand times.

'Only your body is dead, my little mother,' I said to her corpse, with the sleeping face and the folded hands, ignoring the thick bandage around her neck.

'From now on you will be invisibly with me. I beg of you, don't leave me.'

'Come, come,' they whispered behind me, flat and ghostly.

'I wish you could eat these oranges,' I said to her. 'If only I had known yesterday what was in store for us today. I would have – kissed your hands. Yes, I would have. Remember that I promised to buy you a purple blouse so you'd look smashing?'

'Come, come,' they whispered, already with stress.

Noises clattered, insensitive to my loss.

'Goodbye, my little mother,' I said to her for the last time. 'I will see you – when I die.'

They put her in a coffin. At the cemetery I had to look down at the brown box. My ear was where her heart was, hoping still, but the heart stayed silent. I was told to throw a handful of soil on her. I dropped a crumb, and I ached all over when I detached my ear from the silent heart.

'Mary, please help us.' She didn't.

The caretaker of souls was a large man who looked more like the caretaker of coffins. He was the caretaker of the holy book.

'My dear child,' he said and touched me with a large soft hand. I looked at him, but he was not inclined to communicate. I didn't believe in the compassion of his words or his gesture.

'We will leave in two hours,' my uncle said.

I looked up and stared at him as if I had never seen him. He was as distant as a Tasmanian, a Chinaman, a Neanderthal. His eyes held no sorrow for the one in the coffin.

'Two hours,' he said again, and uncovered the watch on his wrist.

He was two hours ahead. Oh, I wasn't. I was years behind. I thought that my mother had always known what I did, felt and thought, that she knew me inside out.

• 16 •

She was long in her coffin, and I was in another city when I still was governed by her.

It is time to get up, Tilly, she said to me in her strict manner.

Eat your soup, Tilly. No matter what, you must eat.

Sometimes only fragments of sentences floated past me. You could hear me whisper, completing the sentence.

What is so fascinating about aeroplanes? she asked. I'd rather watch the birds flying.

Come on down from your cloud, Tilly, or you'll fall hard.

Your head is there for thinking. Try harder.

But she never said that your heart is there for loving.

It was inevitable. As she moved further away, with my uncle's voice choking her voice, she was transformed in my mind. She became a person without me. Arrived on her own, departed on her own.

She became a story. Ella was a country child who played hare and porcupine in the fields with her brothers. Once at the dinner table she burst out laughing when she should have been solemnly eating her meal. A fist, thumping the tabletop, demanded order. Ella couldn't stop herself and was expelled from the room. She went to the stables and spent the night sleeping against the warm belly of a foal.

I can just see her riding that cart downhill. Crashing into a tree. Trudging home with the pieces. Suspecting the wrath of the patriarch. What mischief, said her father. You'll have to pay for it. No sweets for one year. That will teach you, I hope. And he kept his word. No extenuating circumstances.

Ella, when she was twenty-three, had a man in the dark. He came to her room in the night. He took off her stockings. Your thighs feel as soft as silk, he said. Ella, who wasn't raised on kind words, loved to hear such praise. Her eyes began to shine, and she kissed him. And he spoiled her with easy words. You don't really mean it, she said. I mean it, he answered. When her trust in him had become strong and she thought they were inseparable, he savoured her, like champagne and caviar. The man, who was my father, never returned to her room.

That hour with him decided her future. She waited for continuing bliss. When she had waited a long time in vain, love began to fade from her heart forever.

My spirit had taken possession of the sperm that fought its way into her womb. She hid me under her dress, under loosely falling folds, and a tight girdle, and I came into the world as a surprise to the people who knew her. Except to the man in the dark who survived as the faceless donor of the sperm.

Ella's guilt was never erased.

My uncle and I sat at the table, the casserole between us.

'You're not like your mother,' he said and took the ladle out of my hand. 'You shouldn't always be so smart.'

'Why,' I said, focusing on his bushy eyebrows. 'Would you prefer me to be dumb?'

THE ADOLESCENT

I t is November, but we are ahead of time with the wrapping. It is Easter eggs and other seasonal chocolate delights that are wrapped now. I have settled down with a stack of empty boxes on one side and boxes filled with unwrapped Easter eggs on the other. With one hand I pick the first egg, with the other the tinfoil paper. Then I wrap the egg, smooth the paper, give it a pat and put it away.

I've done this work for a few months now, and my fingers have become quick and supple with the hollow merchandise. These days I'm seldom tempted to eat some of the broken chocolate, pieces that came out too thin and broke at a touch. What riches, I said to myself in the beginning. The management knows that you'll get sick from overconsumption one day. That's why they allow you to gorge yourself.

Wrapping Easter eggs, like most work, is rewarded with a bonus. Quietly I sit on my stool and keep count. At an even number I stop and squint and sigh to myself. When I close my eyes to shut out my surroundings, the eggs in shiny tinfoil paper keep on passing and repassing on a conveyor belt in my mind.

To start again I must push myself, but soon I am submerged again in tinfoil eggs, and like the others I compete. Somehow it seems unavoidable.

When I came to work here I behaved differently. I inserted pauses and I stretched and yawned and muttered. But I soon got the message and stopped expressing myself. I took to stealth. Now every time I'm itchy for a change I slip away to the restroom. I don't care for a bonus. That's a lie. I do care for it, but above all I don't want to be regarded as incompetent. Most women are proud to be fast workers.

On my way to the restroom I make a detour past the floor where the chocolate is produced. What a place that is. Some women handle moulds and buckets full of thick chocolate. Parts of the machinery are coated with chocolate. The floor is waxed with the brown sludge. Chocolate is everywhere. The strong smell of cocoa has crept into every crack in the underground establishment.

When we arrive in the morning, the mixtures are already stirring in large tubs. As we leave in the afternoon, the tubs are still turning. The mixtures are never prepared in our presence; the recipes are a secret.

Once a month, a man walks in with a stopwatch. He stays at a distance. Some of the women, noticing him from the corner of their eyes, feel compelled to increase their speed. The man checks his stopwatch, takes notes and walks away.

I stop at the first conveyor belt, which is connected

---

to the chocolate glazing machine. Four women work there, two at the conveyor belt, the other two behind the glazer. The two on the belt are poking a piece of wire into masses of tiny cubes to prevent them from sticking together. In no time they disappear into the cold storage plant.

'Hi,' I say to the women. 'They look hard to do.'

I don't get an answer. They don't look up, and their teeth are clenched with eagerness. It's like watching a battle, chocolate masses against women.

'I haven't done these yet,' I tell them. They keep on poking.

At the other end, with the glazer between them, the two women pour the sweets from a flat wooden box onto the rocker grating and afterwards straighten the heaps into an even layer, before they pass through the glazer. The chocolate flows through a large tube from one of the turning tubs nearby. Since the glazer is chiefly a glass container, the level of the chocolate can be checked at a glance.

The speed of the conveyor belt is suddenly accelerated by one of the women at the rocking grater, with the result that the women at the other end try to adjust to a faster speed. Eventually one of them slackens. She is the older one. Wiping her forehead she misses out on a cluster of sweets. She pretends that she is at ease but is suddenly overwhelmed again by her sense of duty. I open my mouth, expecting her to cry out. But she doesn't. I meet her eyes when she lifts her head. No sign of recognition. Erect she is broad chested, a tall woman aware of her authority. Without rushing she leaves her place and walks over to the other side of the chocolate glazer.

'Turn the speed down, we can't keep up,' she yells.

The woman responsible is not intimidated. She throws back her head, runs to the belt and looks furiously at the running cubes and the remaining woman who hovers above the conveyor belt. Waving her arms, she jumps back to the other side and positions herself in front of the complaining woman. She is thin and small.

'No,' she bellows over the noise of the machines. 'No, I will not turn the speed down. There is a big bonus on them. I'm not going to miss out on that.'

Her cramped white face is cold with determination and to show her intent she leaps over the stack of boxes of sweets and demonstratively empties one out on the grater.

'There you are,' she cries triumphantly. 'Get on with it.'

The elderly woman shakes her head. She raises an arm but then drops it in resignation. 'You are inconsiderate,' she says in a steady voice.

'Get lost,' the temperamental woman craws, her chin and elbows at a sharp angle.

I turn away to hurry back to my own job. The hours pass slowly. At one stage I think I must go for a walk again, but I don't. I seem to be glued to my stool. The ache is back that announces itself somewhere deep in my body.

• 18 •

There are things that can make your life rich and beautiful, like eating chocolate, I once said from the height of some noble assumption.

O mother where are you now?

The big door of the store-room is wide open. Light is streaming in, and I tumble towards it like a moth. I hold my face up and unlock my lips, sinking into the golden arms of the sun. As the sigh of relief evaporates, I have shed the surplus weight. The hard-earned crust will taste sweet.

When I leave the chocolate world, I advance very slowly, to give myself back to myself. Yet parts of me cannot be released. Before my mind's eye tinfoil-papered eggs are passing and repassing, one thousand four hundred of them.

Tomorrow my feet will take me back to the factory, and there my hands will take over, detached from my own free will. Part of my brain is constantly engaged with chocolate masses that follow me wherever I go, a thick brown stream, touching the borders of my retreat, my resort of happiness.

I come home to my radio, a small transistor. I bought it for its convenience, to put it under my pillow or take it wherever I go. I throw myself on the bed and put my legs up against the wall, the radio on my chest. The singer's voice goes straight to my heart. He is the dream-maker, and I am the girl who is winding her way through the flower beds. I am lithe. My feet know no tiredness. The dress I'm wearing is made of white voile, with a flower garland around the hem and sleeves that open up into butterfly wings.

The song has come to an end. Another feeling settles, relying on memory. My uncle comes to the fore, taxing me. I pick up his letter from the bedside table. 'You can come back any time, Tilly,' I read, 'I won't hold it against you that you ran away, but I can't help you with money. Love Uncle Eddi.'

I had written to him out of a sense of homesickness. Memory had begun to paint a picture of him that evaded the ugliness. But I hung on for the truth.

I weighed each word of his letter against my thoughts and feelings, past and present. Love? The old tyrant was never loving. His voice was like a hammer. 'You ungrateful thing,' he hissed from under his moustache, trembling with a peculiar excitement that gave his eyes a steely shine.

'Things?' I echoed, and my spine and collarbone tightened like a bow. I stared him out.

Sometimes I wished that death had taken him away instead of my tailor uncle. But maybe that was unfair to my mother who probably preferred his company to uncle Eddi's. The pair of them, were they smiling at me from out of their immaterial world? Sometimes I felt that this was the case, though it may have been wishful thinking.

Uncle Eddi kept five chickens in his backyard. I chased them to take my frustration out on them. Feathers flew, but it was only on the surface that I enjoyed the insanity of their fear. 'Why don't you drop dead, uncle Eddi, you tough old thing. See what you did. You taught me to be cruel.'

One night I ran away to save my sense of self-respect. Uncle Eddi had begrudged me my food again. Our quarrels were offensive to me, but he thought nothing of them. My escape was planned. It had taken me a year to save the money for the train trip, food and the rent for a room for four weeks.

The first night it was the park for me which was peopled with strange creatures. I rather sensed them than saw them. Their features were vague, animal-like, but they didn't attack me. They were the outcasts of society, vagabonds. Perhaps they were used to youngsters sleeping in their park. Early in the morning I walked mannerly to the railway station. This is what I must do, isn't it, mother? I thought, and I felt that she approved of it.

It is three months later now. Deep autumn. If someone should ask me if I regret my step I'd say no. Two thirds of my time I am free to think how to improve on the other third.

At six I'm going out to buy myself something to eat. On my way back my heel comes off and looking around I see a park bench. Sit down, says the park bench. I walk over and take a seat. Lifting the lid of the warm container, chicken smells fan my nose and tempt my taste buds. I help myself to a drumstick and slowly sink my teeth in it. Fleetingly I think of the rooster with the shimmering feathers and the boy who killed him.

The bench, not far from the footpath, faces the park that has been squeezed in between high-rise buildings, altars of power and industry. Giants who threaten my ideas and question my abilities. What have I to throw in to become high and mighty? Am I just a rooster-loving, chicken-eating manual worker? What will be my future?

The lights over yonder climbing up in the sky, outshine the stars. It is a breathtaking thought that worlds can be set up that expand and swallow up smaller worlds.

My mother and I lived in a world of our own, a pauper's world, while right next to us the twentieth century was hurrying past, ignoring us, going for impossible achievements, achieving them. My mother was daunted by the mighty domes of the new world that belong to those who are fearless of God and the Devil.

Where am I going? Mother? God? Someone? Soon the century will come to an end. I am trying to catch up with the world that is still new to me. I too am daunted by the steep domes and the might that is built on money.

The air is heavy with moisture. Drops trying to hang to the branch of the bush next to me eventually gather into one big drop and slip away. Fog appears from behind a tree in the distance. I imagine giants and goblins roaming about, and spirits of the river rising from the water.

All day I walk around in a trance, the mood changing. It isn't a lack of sleep. I am thinking of Rapunzel, identifying with her.

I know only a few people, I can count my friends on one hand. It doesn't bother me. I am happy with the few I know.

A man with a crunching stride slows down and enters my shaded view. The giants and goblins retreat. The man gapes at me, and says, 'Why are you sitting in the dark all by yourself?'

'Because it suits me.'

'That's queer.'

'That's my worry,' I reply and remember the real

reason why I stopped here. 'My heel came off my shoe.'

'I can fix your heel,' he says quickly. He is eager. He speaks with a hungry voice, to be of service beyond the repair.

'Thank you kindly,' I say drily, acknowledging my body's signals. They tell me that I am eager too. And why? Today is a queer day. I am nostalgic, moody and weak, running from the chocolate stream.

I manage to elicit a smile. Confident enough for him to think I am okay. He responds. A slow smile extends from the corners of his mouth and from there into his eyes. On the spur of the moment I decide to break the monotony of my day. I will take him home with me. One last glance at the high-rise giants. I feel I must challenge my fate.

'Wow,' he says close behind me as I limp ahead on uneven soles, ignoring his surprise.

My house is a maze with dozens of rooms and uncountable floors above my room. The gurgle from radios, record players and televisions hit us the moment we enter.

'Wow,' says the man behind me, poking his finger into his ear.

'Indulgences,' I say, as I fling my bag on the table and turn to face him fully.

'Wow,' he says again, looking around my room, pointing at a row of dolls on the bed.

'My children.' I introduce them.

'Christ,' he says when our eyes meet. 'You have unusual eyes. You remind me of – '

'Never mind that.' I interrupt his attempt to cut the tedious story short. 'I would like you to fix my heel.

I'll go and get a hammer and nails.'

When the heel is fixed I say, 'And now I want to thank you. I don't expect you to do it for nothing.' I pause in preparation for what I am going to say, and I look at him closely, but apart from his features I can't see anything in him that rouses my curiosity. Besides, if I want to oblige my body's desire, I'll have to be bold.

My thoughts go astray, to take into account any objectors, but there is no one to deter me, no voice. Veiling my inner self, I avoid thinking of my mother.

'I am eighteen years old,' I say proudly. 'I have never made love to anyone. When you came along I thought – Oh never mind what I thought – Right or wrong who can tell in advance.'

I pause for effect, hold my breath. He may be the obstacle. But no fear, the light in his eyes pilots me into total freedom of speech.

'I can see that you'd like to make love to me.'

The critical moment has arrived. I stretch myself tall and take off all my clothes, shoes first. Standing there in an awkward pose I feel like a featherless bird.

He looks at me as I would look at a juicy ham in a delicatessen shop, not the way I look at David or Bacchus.

I close my eyes for the fall. Landing is hard. Keep my eyes closed, holding on to my soul. Don't like being clamped in. One eye opens to peep, focusing filament in globe. Hymen is broken. Moan not. Light is thick. He rides the sea. Underneath dreams go on. David is it you? Bacchus, my love, it should have been you. Come on top of me, Lorenzo. Jesus, be mine! Steam is coming off him. He rolls along without me, in silence.

After he has made love to me, I sit up and look at him straight. 'I didn't like it at all.'

He blushes. His arms hang down, his eyes are on me in an incomprehensible question. 'Why not?' he asks, with effort.

'How would I know,' I say. 'I've never done it before. But I thought it would be different.'

'We've just met,' he says. 'We could try again. It might be better for you next time.'

'No, thank you.' I shake my head. 'I don't think you're right for me.'

'Can I wash myself?' he asks, lifting his shoulders.

I like his shoulders. They could shoulder a portal. A Florentine portal. O David, O Brutus. I still love you.

'Go ahead,' I say, disenchanted. I get up to get him a fresh towel and get back on the bed.

'We could try again,' he says through the running water. His voice has regained certainty.

'I tried,' I say, thumping my belly with my fist, 'and I didn't like it. I actually hated it. Yeah.' I stop drumming my belly. 'You have the wrong smell.'

'The wrong what?' he says, stepping into his trousers.

'Wrong smell,' I say, putting my underpants on.

He stands there staring. A stranger. A fucker at my wish.

'I suggest you go home now,' I say moodily. 'I'd like to read.'

He sits down, motionless for a while. I peer at my books, stacked up in piles on the floor. I haven't got a bookshelf.

'I like your smell,' he says. 'You smell sweet, like chocolate.'

'La-la-la,' I fume. 'Tiss-tiss-tiss. Are you leaving or aren't you? If not, can you tell me a story?'

'Story? What story? What kind of a demand is that? You're not serious, are you? – You are? – I'm not a storyteller, you know.'

'You take things literally,' I say. 'If you have nothing to say, why don't you go home?'

All I want now is to be alone and think about what I have done, was it of any significance.

'You're crazy,' he says, 'absolutely crazy.'

'Thanks. I appreciate your opinion of me.'

'Christ,' he says, rising from his chair and moving towards the door. Once more he turns around hissing his disapproval. I am not going to change his mind. Before he vanishes I memorize his features. His face is round, his eyes are brown. He is much too pretty. I should have picked an ugly man.

'God bless you,' I say loudly against the closed door. The voice coming back to me has abandoned all pretence.

I sink into immobility.

Trickles of violin music find their way to me, trailed by a chorus singing aaaaaaah.

Apart from my underpants I am still naked. For a long time I meditate on the big red spot almost in the middle of the crumpled bedspread.

'It's okay,' I say aloud. Maybe my little mother can hear me, she who believed that the blood she spent on my father was special. I don't think it is special. I only wonder why the entrance to a woman is blocked in that way.

One day our brand of biscuits might rank among the top ten. Who cares, really? It wouldn't make any difference to the workers. Wages are never affected by the increasing wealth of a single company.

The factory comprises one large rectangular building, the sections interconnected without being divided by walls. The bakery is set up at one end, the packing department at the other. Then there is the weighing and storing department, and beside some smaller departments a fair portion of space is taken up by tins that have been returned from the retailers. They will be relabelled, once the old labels have been removed with spatulas; then the tins will be transported to the labelling department. The old labels are scraped off when there is a lull in the production of biscuits.

Lengthwise the hall is divided by a baking-oven-machine attached to a conveyor belt of considerable length.

Every morning we line up in a certain order beside the conveyor belt. A dozen women are positioned behind a rack on which a biscuit tin is placed obliquely. Stacks of tins from the labelling department are lined up beside the racks.

Another dozen women, closer to the oven, are positioned behind a small table, its purpose being to hold a simple shelved wooden box and a narrow metal container which holds a certain number of biscuits. Beside their tables only a small number of tins are stacked. They will hold the ready packets.

Soon the heat rises from the gargantuan belly of the oven, mingling with the heat of the sun pounding on the roof.

Some women carry jugs of iced water from a tap in the baking department, distributing them on the extra wrapping tables within reach. Some women refresh themselves with Coca Cola. Already our proper white uniforms show dark patches of perspiration.

Last preparations are made before the biscuits roll out. It takes fifteen minutes, during which the biscuits glide through the oven, like an army of soldiers advancing on a battlefield.

Everyone stands at attention, ready to dig into the flood of biscuits which now appear in the oven's mouth. Our eyes focus on like a radar eye. And all conversation ceases.

As soon as the biscuits are out, the first women bend over to gather handfuls, and though they are red hot they don't take much notice. Their mind is set on speed and bonus.

By the time the biscuits are ready to be packed, hands are all over the conveyor belt in a shoving gesture, clearing the battlefield fast.

The second woman on the right has worked twelve years in the biscuit factory.

'Look at her,' the other women whisper, but she wouldn't hear them if they shouted. Her face is devoid of expression. With one quick grip she gathers the exact number of biscuits needed for a packet. No biscuits slip through her fingers. No counting is needed. She has developed a separate sense. She is finely tuned, responding to the conveyor belt that pushes the biscuits in front of her nose. She must take responsibility. Her arms at an angle, she swings to and fro. Her head starts spinning, then her shoulders. She rotates to the rhythm of her wrapping fingers, reliable instruments. Not once does she balk.

At the end of the session she stares vacantly at the virtually empty conveyor belt until she realizes her backwardness and gradually unwinds. After she takes her full tins to the weighing department, she stoically walks to the restroom, gets out her sandwiches and begins to eat.

Only seldom is she drawn into the chatter around her, and then only for a personal reason. She will spot a new face. 'You're new here?' she'll say and continue without waiting for an answer. 'I've been here for donkey's years. My son is going to be a doctor. I'm saving up for his education.' That's the point she wants to make.

She keeps on talking about her favoured subject. Her limbs begin to rotate, her head is spinning. Her astonished listener soon turns away.

Ahead of anyone else the woman returns to the conveyor belt, to prepare for a fresh lot of biscuits. Walking past the baking oven, she sees the supervisor pushing tins around at the far end of the hall.

The supervisor has worked twenty-five years in the biscuit factory, since it was founded. They promoted her to the position ten years ago. Her authority though is restricted to the women. The few men at the top work independently.

Favouritism has no chance with the woman. The management sees her as an integral part of the factory. Her breathing and thinking is biscuits, and although she knows fifteen kinds intimately, she knows nothing about us, with the exception of the son of the rotating woman.

She rushes her tea breaks. She is constantly busy, walking around with a writing pad, pushing tins around with her foot, lining them up in the weighing department, counting the full tins and those to be re-labelled, carrying cartons, writing daily reports. A few times during the day she walks over to the spot where a new filling machine is installed to oversee its efficiency.

The machine, a new design, proves to be a problem. Almost every day it breaks down. The engineer has to be called, and he arrives with an assistant and a screwdriver. Thoughtful remarks are exchanged between the men about the cause of the standstill, while the woman who is in charge of the machine respectfully stands aside and listens.

Occasionally one of the pastry cooks joins them. He is no expert in these matters either and is silent, but when the experts have left he gives his opinion.

'That machine not only looks like a toy,' he says, 'but is as short lived as one.'

The supervisor nods, gives an agreeable laugh, and they go about their business again.

Meanwhile the biscuits are filled by hand by four women using a nozzle.

At the end of the day, when the last worker has left, the supervisor checks that everything is switched off. She walks about, prolonging her stay. Satisfied she listens to the hum of the Coca Cola fridge and inhales the lingering smell of the dough at the top end of the hall. Otherwise there is silence.

She punches her card, puts it back into one of the wall shelves and nods at the office girl in her glass box.

Outside she looks up at the sky and while she fills her lungs with fresh air she repositions her shoulders. Walking down the grounds in front of the factory she focuses on the bus stop. All the women have gone from there, and that's how she prefers it.

• 20 •

She passes me by in the crowd. Directing her steps carefully to avoid a collision, she doesn't take notice of anything but the continuous pressure from all sides. Her feeble shoulders are vaulted over her breasts, almost burying them. Like everyone else, she is weaving her way through obstacles, assuming a posture of defence in the thicket, rising and falling in the tide of human bodies.

She never had wings, the old spinster, she was never young.

'Miss Edith.' The men point their fingers against their temples to greet her. While Miss Nestle nods she looks at the floor and slips past them as if they were fire and she were afraid of getting burned.

Close to her thigh, rocked by its rhythm, dangles an imitation leather handbag in the higher price range. She wears a grey skirt, though grey is not in fashion right now. The blue of her blouse is uncertain, doused by a formal grey. Under her chin, between the tips of the collar, nestles a tiny bow. But you know that she didn't buy the blouse for its cheeky bow but to match the practical skirt.

Sometimes her head jerks aside when the sun darts through her spectacles, and I part my lips to greet her.

Something is occupying her mind. Her mother is waiting impatiently. 'You're late, Edith. You know I don't like to be on my own.'

'Yes, mother, I know.' It's no use telling her about the distractions on the way and the freedom that lies in walking about.

'You don't know what it means to be a cripple.'

'No, mother,' Edith agrees. She turns aside and bends across to the budgerigars. Heavenly messengers, Edith thinks. With pointed lips she whispers pleasantries to her little darlings. Her extended finger coaxes them with tenderness. A smile settles on her unlovely lips, but before it deepens the old woman leans forward urgently and holds out an arm. 'Help me with the potty.'

'Yes, mother.'

I let Edith Nestle slip away. I'm in no hurry to go home. Shop windows draw me close, and my heart grows fond of the things that make you look beautiful – the silky blouse, the luscious négligé, the pearls and the thick golden bracelets. Lost in admiration I hit my forehead on the glass. It sobers me up, and I sniff the biscuit smell that hangs in my hair.

The women chattered and laughed when they changed in the dressing-room. It was payday, the best day of the week. Shedding their sweaty uniforms, they stood in their slips, their breasts accentuated with pink, white, blue, or creamy lace. Smooth cheeks their attraction, tufts of hair, bare armpits, big bosoms like foam cushions, mixed smells of sweat and roll-on deodorant. I leered at them like a Peeping Tom.

The twitter of their voices was untiring. They thought of what to cook for dinner and whether to watch television or do some sewing long put off.

Rossana, with her big mouth, announced loudly that tonight she was going to get laid; she needed it badly, being close to her period. No one answered her. Suddenly they were busy with their zippers, stuffing things into their handbags. Most of them were married.

'You're coy or something?' Rossana laughed, filling the gap of embarrassment. 'They're coy.' She answered her own question.

I felt admiration for her who moved like a lioness among domestic cats.

Even the girl with the contemptuous bearing had improved. In the morning she had let the biscuits run by, picking up two or three at a time, putting them in the tin in slow motion, taking more interest in watching the scraping hands on the conveyor belt. Her nostrils flared with disdain when she looked at the record wrapper.

I looked up from the other side of the belt, abandoning my eagerness to keep up with the others. My smile, I hoped, wasn't apologetic.

Spitefully, she squashed a few biscuits, opened her hand and dropped the crumbs. 'I hate it.'

'Oh, Celia,' I said, pulling a face.

'It's appalling,' she groaned.

The biscuits flowed past us untouched. I felt

worried about it again and tried to control the reflection of despondency on my face.

'Celia, gosh.' I stoked the fire in her.

'I'm going to quit. As soon as there's a vacancy at Woolworth's, I'm gone.' Another biscuit crushed in her hand.

I nodded at her and considered her my friend.

High above the crowds the sun enters the windows of the high-rise buildings, throwing orange reflections. A window-cleaner sticks to the glass, the size of a pinhead. A paper-seller calls the headlines. About a war. Which one's that? A flower-seller stretches her arm out, offering roses. If I had a lover he would bring me roses.

The city is under the stampede of a million feet. My head is foggy. My fingers burn. Want to lick them like a dog licks his wound. Curse hot biscuits. I make no sound. How brave can you be?

I am going home to my radio. Sedately.

Loud voluptuous music showers down on me as I enter the house, flowing down the staircase, flirting with Hollywood vampishness.

Ah, I am soft again, like an over-ripe peach, ready to drop into the picker's hand. Hope his hand will not be calloused. The music splashes through the orifices, surges against the glands.

My door is the second on the left on the ground floor. A long narrow window opens to the street. I push the key in the keyhole and turn around for a voice.

'Hello, young lady,' the old man says. A step too

close, he establishes himself in front of me. He giggles, poking at the buttons of my blouse.

I stare at him, peach that I am, and he totters away on his calcified legs. In front of his door he turns.

'You should go out more often, girlie, and have a good time.'

Sometimes I do, seduced by the throbbing night lights that undermine my good intentions. But the morning after I am resentful.

Thoughts can exude such a stench.

On an ardent evening, when there is no dying in the air, I watch the candle melt on my windowsill. Faces gather behind the glass, but I don't draw the curtain. I stare back at them, the candle between us, an invisible barrier.

The eyes on the other side open wide, suck me in. Noses nod at me and peck. People out there want to know why I sit here like a statue drained of life. What is the matter, woman behind the candle?

Nothing is the matter. No matter. Nothing. Mother?

Blow out the candle, Flaxen-head.

Mother, my mother has come.

I blow out the candle, and giggle. A hand paws the window pane. Howling, whistling and squeaking outside.

Animals, my mother says.

Peaches, I think.

Summer is long, like the ocean wave that travels between two continents . You ride the wave, arms spread out for balance, irregularities met in the bent knees. You ride the wave forever.

In my dream I walk into the factory. I sit down on

the conveyor belt that transports me back to the mouth of the baking oven. As I approach the hot hole, I cringe, but the suction pulls me forward and I scream as my hands get flattened.

• 21 •

Today I realize how prejudiced I was when I had my first affair, but it must be said that the manuals don't tell you anything about behaviour – whether you should express your thoughts and feelings, whether you should refrain from saying anything, or if it is wise to say something favourable even if it is a lie. They don't define what love is, to what degree it is important, what the effects are, to what depths it can lead, and whether it depends on caressing or caressing on love.

The examples offered are theoretical and illustrated with astonishing pictures of positions, some of which frighten and repel me. There is one picture in particular. The woman stands on her hands, the man stands upright behind her. I can imagine her gasping for air, and I can hear her begging for a change of position. You wonder what she gets out of it, and why she is doing it. Speaking for myself, I can say that I will never agree to standing on my hands during love-making.

What I need is some sensible advice.

One day I asked Rossana. We had met in the washroom. No one else was around. Coconut biscuits were on; easy to handle. There was no hurry for us to go back.

'Rossana,' I said, 'I need some advice.'

'What is it, kid?' She brushed her hair, but she

looked as if she felt the brush all over her body. She'd be the right one to ask, I thought.

'I'm inexperienced – I don't know how you go about things. I don't know what to say and how to behave. I feel so uncertain, so clumsy and inarticulate when it comes to love-making. What do you say when you make love?'

'Say, behave?' she returned my question.

'Yes,' I waved my hand, 'exactly that.'

Her brush didn't stop.

'I don't know,' she said, 'you just do it.'

'Isn't that crude? The elephants and the bower birds have such a wonderful preliminary round before they get down to it.'

'Elephants?' she squealed.

'Forget it,' I said. But I couldn't leave it alone. 'Rossana, come on, tell me.'

She was putting on mascara and looked at me with one eye done up. 'I just do it.'

'You just let it happen?'

'Something like that.'

'You lie back and close your eyes? Are you active or passive?'

'Active and passive.'

'What are most men like?'

'They're okay.'

'What does that mean?'

She shrugged.

'Do they all melt into one?'

She had almost finished her face, tapping it here and tapping it there, as if to improve on her natural features. 'Funny way of putting it, but I suppose that's it.'

'There must be something more to it?'

'If you're crazy about a guy, yes.'

'What does that do?'

'You want to do it all the time.'

Rossana had finished with me and left. She was a beautiful girl but disappointing to me. Her beauty, I thought, was only on the outside.

If my mother were still alive I couldn't have asked her either. She wouldn't have known what sensible advice was.

The cafe off the beaten track is one of my favourite places. The proprietor collects clocks, with which he decorates the walls.

I am extremely fond of cakes, and the ones you get here are out of this world. They are works of art, not only for the eye but for the tongue and the heart.

Which brings me to another reason for coming here. I like to observe the young couples for whom this is the perfect place for a stimulating conversation and an underhand flirt.

Today a man sits opposite me at the next table gazing at me indiscriminately, without moving a muscle.

His face is square and rather immobile. There are pinch pleats at the corner of his mouth. Maybe he is working too hard or going through a divorce. He doesn't seem to be waiting for anyone.

Occasionally our eyes meet, and I wonder what Rossana would do in my place. There are a few single men in the room, but my eyes keep returning to the man opposite me, and as he begins to appeal to my imagination, I invent a name and a life for him. The couples who entwine their legs under the table and touch with a finger are forgotten.

A picture comes between us. Near the dark side of a house, beside a wooden fence, we sink to the ground. His body rolls on top of me like a rock. I moan. He has no voice. Suddenly it is over, and I recoil and sulk.

The man with the square face stares intently. I blush for what I've been thinking and hide behind the gesture, hand brushing across the cheek. But then it is tucked away under the table, clamped between the thighs.

This is a new beginning. I will tell you my secrets. I would like to give you my heart. How will it be in your arms? If you feel one way and I the other, how do we get it to match? Between us is an empty room with opposite doors. We stand in the doorway. Are we going to move in together?

I am displeased with myself for being hasty again when the clocks go off, one after the other.

I've had enough coffee and cake. Two doughnuts and two pieces of chocolate cake. With two cups of coffee. No crumb left that could keep me. The only thing to do is to leave. As I get up and take my shoulder bag, his eyes shift with my move. I walk away. His eyes follow me. I can feel them on my hips, and in the playfully swinging folds of my skirt.

He has returned to the cafe. Probably only because he likes cakes as much as I do, or because the cafe serves the best doughnuts in town.

I twinkle to greet him but nothing happens. The situation is exactly as it was two days ago. Before I sit down I look at my favourite clock, acknowledge the two couples who look into each other's eyes, and huddle myself into a feeling of comfort and indulgence.

The man I like rubs his chin. His name could be Bruno. What is it that bothers you? Your wife? Your love? Or your obsession? His hand is attractive. If I can't tell what goes on in his head, I can tell by his hand some delicate disposition.

The unoccupied room is still there, waiting to be occupied. It is odd. I don't see unoccupied rooms with everyone. Bruno rubs his chin, in soft slow circles, persistent with questions.

Three pieces of cake and my third cup of coffee. I feel slightly sick, but I would like to see how long he can last.

A brain is a peculiar thing. I don't think that mine belongs to me, only that I am allowed to occupy it and follow its notions. I can never fathom the tips of the roots down there at the bottom. Perhaps it isn't Bruno I want. Why not when he is here right in front of me, rubbing his chin?

I can't stand it. I'm trapped, like I'm in an elevator that is stuck. I want to behave outrageously. Shout or sing. But instead of dropping my cup or performing a stunt I clench my fist and lower my head. I am a civilized person. Don't do that, my mother said.

Away from sight, under the table, my feet are not so obedient. Tap tap tap, they go. How silly is Tilly. Wasting her time.

At the door I turn and throw a blazing look at the

man who still rubs his chin. I can't be bothered. My heart is light in my chest when I reach the wide open spaces again.

Bruno's name is George. His wife had left him. He worked for an insurance company.

The next time I saw him I was already sitting over my cake and coffee. He walked in. Walk is an understatement. He stormed into the place as if he was late for an appointment. I moved like a blade of grass under the wind.

Standing in front of my table he asked if he could sit down in the other chair.

'It is not my chair,' I said. I was pink with pleasure.

'Have you already had your three pieces of cake?' he asked humorously.

'No. Oh, you've noticed?'

He arranged his medium-size frame on the chair, his elbows on the table. His eyes were brown. His pinch pleats had gone. His face unsmiling. I tried a Buddha smile.

In a while he talked about insurance, later about his wife. Gradually he began to fill in the sketch I had made of him. I saw my hand unfurl on the tablecloth, one finger pointing in his direction. He tapped his fingers or let them lie sleeping together.

The waitress's arms came between us. She put down a cup, but I don't know in front of whom. Another look across the room.

'It's getting late.' The statement put the ground back under my feet. My suggestion didn't come spontaneously. I had it figured out before he came in today, and I had no difficulty presenting it to him. I wanted him to come home with me, but I would not be hasty. My home was my pride. A bookcase had been added to my possessions, two large cushions, another teddybear and some decorative objects.

He nodded. On our way we walked as if we were going through a narrow tunnel filled with warm moist air, not too far apart. Soon my house came in sight.

'I only rent a room,' I said, to prepare him. 'Where do you live?'

'In a flat,' he said.

'Lucky you!' I opened the door as wide as it would go and invited him in with a flourish.

A smile softened his face making it round. I'd asked him to sit down on the floor on one of the new cushions. At the flick of a switch music blasted from the radio. Why on earth did it have to be brass music? I changed the station. As I move back from the radio, my left knee touched him. Where was the spark, the famous spark? Was it hidden deep?

'Have you read all these books?' he asked.

'Most of them.'

'Hm,' he said.

'Do you read books?'

'Sometimes,' he said languidly.

He was slow. Books weren't his subject. Impatiently I pounced on the radio again. The music had stopped and was followed by a political discussion.

'We don't want that, do we?' I said. 'War, abduction, assassination, it's too much.'

He smiled again and sat like a person who appreciates home life. Almost like a father. Perhaps that was his attraction.

'The first time I saw you you wore a blue dress,' he said, 'and your hair was blown and tangled. It was a windy day. The second time your hair was nicely combed and you looked as if you had just come out of the bath.'

I looked at the floor, relishing the hum in his voice, without being distracted by his features. 'Ah, really? A blue dress? I can't remember.'

'Look,' he said, pointing, 'someone at the window.'

I jumped up to close the curtain. Like silk I slithered back on the cushion in front of his feet. Don't do that, I thought, but didn't change my position.

He looked down on me with the eyes of an older man. 'You're very young,' he said.

'I don't like being very young.'

'I like it.'

'Why?'

'Youth is admirable.'

'Do you admire me?'

'Yes.'

'It doesn't do anything for me. I'd rather be experienced like you. How old are you?'

'Thirty-three.'

'That's nothing. I won't feel old when I'm thirty-three. I think I'll feel enriched but not envious of a younger person.'

We stopped talking. He stretched out his hand and wrapped it around my wrist and kissed the inside of my hand. It was nice, but did he expect me to melt now? Was the question visible on my forehead, and my lips disdainful? Tilly, you are impossible, I said to myself and closed my eyes on the observer, to receive the next kiss, the important kiss on the lips.

The kiss began. I flinched. Saliva came between us ousting good will. I remembered my mother's spittle.

My mouth retracted. His saliva was flowing. I couldn't stop thinking how I disliked it, that I would like to push him away and hit him and burst out in a tantrum. If I didn't want to drink his saliva, I had to let it run. Oh, he was insensitive not to notice. His mouth was licking, sucking, slobbering with a passion I didn't share.

My dislike grew into hate. It locked my hands into fists. I pushed and my hate exploded like dynamite.

Astonished eyes looked at me, as if he were innocent. Not to do further damage I smiled. No. It was a lieing smile. Why was it I who felt embarrassed?

I spat into my jumper and wiped away his saliva. He watched me. His annoyance grew, demanding an apology.

'Sorry.' I boxed the cushion. It was a lie. I was not sorry. At the back of my mind I knew that if he continued to kiss me in that way it would be the end of our relationship.

'I would prefer it if you didn't produce so much moisture.' Has anyone ever complained about a first kiss?

He didn't answer. He sat back on the cushion. 'I never sit on cushions,' he said.

'Sit on the chair or the bed.'

He chose the chair. Looking at the dolls his face

emptied of expression. He began to escape the room.

'I'll make a coffee.' I whistled while I made the coffee, to fill the pause that stretched between us.

Taking the cup to him and kissing him on the forehead I erased our differences.

His smile was just a poor flicker. Drinking the coffee he didn't have to look at me.

I touched him with a finger. 'I do like you.'

'And I like you.'

We talked for a while about it and were united again. Then I led him to the door and there I took the initiative. It would be 'my' kiss. I was hopeful. After all that I suppose it was a childish kiss, frugal and economical. But it was clear and cleansing.

'Goodnight.' I held out my hand. It was a gesture of friendship.

'Goodnight, love.'

'I'll see you tomorrow,' he said, 'here, at your place.' Waving at me he left the house.

Two months later we ended the affair on a flamboyant note, and the reason for it was banal. Who wants to spend one's precious life in disharmony? Disagreements and the fight for power are usually base, mean and vulgar. I was not the masochist to put up with it.

Still, it wasn't easy. I had to get used to being alone again and learn not to take anyone for granted, as I had George. And it occurred to me that I might stay single. Love or no love, I will have to stay content with my offers.

Apart from relationships I must think of my

future. The change I want will have to be an improvement. Our record-wrapper is an symbol to me of what should not become of a woman.

• 22 •

She hired me straight away. What a relief the change was. I could sit down now, if only for a few minutes at a time. I was never sweaty or dirty again, and I could wear high heels. Wearing a uniform had become unnecessary.

No one can enter or leave the hotel without being seen by me. I was employed because of my eyes. The hotel proprietor was mesmerized when she saw me. 'Your eyes,' she cried and recited one of the phrases I know so well.

Then she sniggered. 'When men look into your eyes, they will be distracted from the price of the room,' she said. My eyes would moderate the price.

I don't mind that the woman is eccentric and that she produces words with the speed of a waterfall, though often after a few minutes of dutiful listening I pray to God to shut her up.

Every morning she comes in flapping like a huge erratic butterfly. I cringe a little knowing where she will land. She takes hold of my hand and investigates my face as if to reassure herself that my eyes are still there.

'Honestly,' she says. The bangles around her wrist clatter, and the ear-rings tremble with conviction. Her mouth shapes into a pink fruity 'O' when she extols her astonishment. I can't be annoyed with her for long. She is so unintentionally funny.

While I report to her the arrivals and departures,

---

handing her money and bills, she walks around with an extended finger, wiping the edges of the furniture. Although she seems more interested in dust than in business matters, I soon discover her talent for remembering sums of money and numbers of guests.

The reception area is the representative part of the hotel, and it has been designed to impress. I am happy watering, feeding and dusting the rubber plants and the palm trees, of which there are four. The wood panelling on two sides is still the genuine stuff. My chair, of course, can swivel.

Sometimes the cook appears at the end of the passage leading to the kitchen, leaning against the wall with one shoulder, one leg wrapped around the other, staring at me.

'Hello, Joe,' I call out to him.

'Hello.' His stare puts a nail through you. He never greets me first. His puffed up hat nods a reply from a proud height. Coal black hair coils around his earlobes. What bothers him is of whom I remind him. Actually I begin to wonder myself.

Joe's tongue was not made for talking but for tasting, and within this field he is an expert and occasionally an artist. One day he handed me his 'Cafe de Paris' sauce recipe and said in an intimate voice, 'Just for you.' But I am not flattered by his admiration. His brooding gaze, like a cold clammy hand, causes my discomfort.

Our hotel is only small. It has seventy-eight single and double rooms and is seldom fully occupied. Some guests have made it their permanent home. At first they think it is convenient to live in a small hotel, that it gives them more privacy than a rented single room. Their linen is changed twice a week, the room is cleaned daily, the soap is free and breakfast is included. They are practically taken care of. Besides they like to think that living in a hotel makes them special.

After a few months, when the novelty has gone, this usually changes. They feel that no one cares whether they are dead or alive, that hotels are impersonal places, that the glamour of being a 'guest' is not really an advantage. Some of them move back into private accommodation.

For a few the hotel becomes a hermitage, a hide-away from others and possibly themselves, to be a stranger among strangers.

One of the guests is a colourless young woman of whom we only know that she is waiting for her husband to return from a war in the east. When she pays her bill, she returns my smile with effort so that I only remark on the weather. The rest of the week she takes no notice of me. One of the housemaids tells me that her room always looks untouched, that not even an envelope lies on the bedside table or in the waste basket.

The other young woman who has permanent residence with us is the exact opposite. The reason she gives for boarding in a hotel is that she can hold parties to which no one objects. (I wonder.) Being indescribably untidy, she is lucky to have a house-maid to clean up after her.

Maybe I should mention the grieving hermit, Karl Krueger, another of our regulars. The day I began working here he came to my desk to introduce himself. From then on he looked upon me as someone he could confide in, but I'm sure he had more than one sympathizer.

'My wife divorced me.' He looked at the electric clock behind me, as if it was his wife and as if she was deceased.

'I'm sorry.'

'My life is in ruins. I am sorry too.'

'Why?' I asked.

'It can't be mended.'

'Time is a great healer.'

He shook his head. Dandruff dropped on his shoulder. He already collects dust, I thought, and turned away not to let him see my grin.

'What do you do when you're not working and don't go anywhere?' I asked.

'I read.'

'Newspapers?'

'Anything.'

'They say if you lose your dog get another one. The same applies to people.'

Karl Krueger was a man with a rigid conception of things, not the marrying kind. The impersonal atmosphere of the hotel suited him perfectly, no demands on his character.

Most people passing through I forget. But I will never forget the small family who arrived yesterday. They walked into the hotel amid the ear-piercing screaming of their baby, who was about two years old. It had the effect of an alarm going off. I jumped up and leaped forward. People appeared, startled, as if they had come out from a shelter. I asked the couple, shouting, if they would like to book in? They shouted back yes.

When the man signed the register, he let go of the child's hand and left it to the mother. The child writhed and struck an even higher note, sounding like a siren. The mother hushed the child and murmured to soothe him, but he was hard to hold, and when she couldn't handle him anymore she began to spank him.

Her face turned crimson and her eyes darkened with anger and embarrassment. The child struck an even higher note, and she turned her back on me, evading my stare and my growing nervousness. Harshly she plucked the child's arm, and perhaps, I thought, it would have relieved her if it would have come off. His limbs boxed in all directions and suddenly he pushed himself back as rigid and straight as an arrow.

Her arms had to be strong to hold him. At the same time she needed to calm him. It seemed impossible. The child continued to scream, and neither his mother's voice nor her plucking and shaking him had the slightest effect. When the man approached to help again he was pushed back by the child's kicking feet and the mother's elbow. Tears came to her eyes when she looked at her husband. Her mouth opened and perhaps she uttered a moan, but it couldn't be heard. The child screamed louder and longer.

The man, thinking an explanation was due, threw his hands in the air. His wild eyes were close in front of me when he shouted, 'He screams day and night. It is hatred, he is full of hate.'

'Why is that?' I shouted back.

'Why is that, why is that?' he babbled irritably with one eye on the baby, as a matter of habit. Screaming and pushing they left the lobby. When they reached the stairs, the hysterical voice of the mother sounded out, 'Be quiet, for God's sake, be quiet. Or I'll – ' Her voice cracked and collapsed.

They were still heard in the next corridor. As soon as the noise faded people began to move again. I let out a sigh of relief and looked at the man's name in the register. The first two letters were normal, the others looked as if they were running away.

In a while a woman came running down the stairs and said, 'Someone is screaming in one of the rooms and won't stop. I've knocked but nobody answers. Do something, for heaven's sake. It's unbearable.'

I left my desk, which I seldom do, and when I knocked on the young couple's door there was no reply, but the screaming went on.

Something had to be done. I had decided to ring the Department of Social Welfare when the screaming stopped. There was an eery silence from behind the door. I knocked again. No answer.

This morning the young family checked out. As they passed by I jumped up from my chair and called out, 'Have you had any breakfast?'

'No,' the woman said hastily. Her foot jerked interrupting the rhythm of her walk. 'We don't want any.' Her voice was small and husky, her eyes avoided directness.

Strange, I thought, why don't they want any breakfast?

The man said nothing, just looked ahead. Passing by, they walked at the far side of the corridor instead

of in the middle. He carried the child, the woman the
suitcase. The child's head rested against his shoulder, its trunk leaned peacefully against his chest.
One hand gently supported the child's head. His
eyes were closed, his face waxen. In a fleeting
moment during which I noticed that my hand was
raised as if to hold them back and ask them curious
questions, I felt that the peacefulness of the bundle
in his arm was deceptive.

The next minute they were gone, but the picture of
them was still in my mind's eye. I could see them
walking on and on, riding buses and trains on a
never-ending journey. The eyes of the child were
closed all the time in a deep unearthly sleep.

A small noise, a thud, returns me to my swivel chair.
Looking up, I see an orange rolling across the desk
towards me.

'Stop looking gloomy,' the grieving hermit says.
He waves his arm. I catch half a headline from the
folded newspaper. Attack on the Mo – . He is off to
work.

I peel the orange. I swallow segment after segment
until the orange is gone. I wipe my hands from the
sticky juice and clear the puzzle from my mind. The
sleeping child is part of two distraught people who
carry it silently from place to place. The orange and
the child don't exist anymore.

• 23 •

His name is Carter. He lives, it seems, high in the
clouds, at his feet an enchanting view. You can sit by

the window for hours watching the pigeons coming and going on the dome's square and the river reflecting the old buildings like an old pewter mirror. In the water that carries their picture so lightly they are ruffled and blurred, they ripple and dissolve.

The two colours of the river are a light and dark grey, never a shade of blue. As the river approaches the city centre, its medieval heart, it becomes a dignified companion of the buildings alongside.

The city authorities wouldn't dare allow the noble decaying structures to be pulled down to make way for rational architecture. They are the essence of human endeavour and survival. Flocks of pigeons glide softly about them, tying invisible bows to them. Their affection for the place is obvious and passed on to the observer, but while I follow their flight with my eyes I feel as if past and present are alloyed and I am immortal.

'Isn't it charming?' Carter says, his face next to mine, watching a pigeon which is spinning an elegant bow and fastening it to a small blind window at the side of the dome. His fingertip stays for a while on the windowsill under the pigeon. 'Isn't it wonderful?'

'Wonderful you,' I reply with a sweep of my arm, meaning to include the pigeons, the river, those dignified buildings and all that is in contact with him every minute of the day.

He squeezes my hand and his lips touch my temple.

'Likewise,' he says and reverses his attention to the picturesque view in front of us. 'You never get tired of a view like this,' he says. 'Timelessness is a wonderful state of mind.'

'You are a wonderful state of mind,' I say. Every word Carter says is special.

A Kokoschka reproduction adorns one of his walls. 'I particularly like its abundance of colour,' he says, transferring his affectionate look from the print to me.

'Yes, Carter,' I nod. I can't take my eyes off him, neither my hands. He has to do something to break the spell.

'You're crazy,' he says fondling my ear.

'Yes, Carter,' I admit, 'but isn't it wonderful?'

He laughs, a soft chuckle, and I feel pleased about it, content to my toes.

Seldom now I think of the other men, number one, two, three and four. Carter will be no number. He is deserving.

Carter is ten years my senior and a little like a father and a little like a brother. When he sits in his shabby chair, he grows silent. While I talk, he keeps his eyes on me. His eyes are deep and provocative, constantly pushing me to talk about myself, about what I think and the most unimportant things. I tip out everything that is inside my head before him, like a box full of toys. Sometimes I sound like a conceited talebearer and though he doesn't object, he doesn't ever try to outsmart me.

'I've had twenty men already.' I pick the number because it comes into my head.

'Oh yes?' he says, without emphasis on the question.

'Yes,' I say emphatically, distorting the uninteresting remark further. 'I always fell for men with small, narrow eyes.'

'Is that so?' he says. But he is not impressed. He kisses the top of my head.

'Did you ever specialize when choosing a woman?'

'No.'

'Your eyes aren't particularly small.'

'Have you changed your mind about the size, then?'

'Yes, and about time,' I say gleefully, glibly.

'Come closer. Closer.' I cup his head with my hands and push it down into my lap. He twists into a comfortable position. I wouldn't make a sound even if my thighs went numb with the weight of him.

Carter says, 'Once when I was a boy I blew up a frog. He burst. The picture still haunts me.'

'Don't worry about it. I'm sure it wasn't the prince in disguise.' I laugh. No moral indignation like I had for the boy who killed the rooster.

Carter wrinkles his forehead. Two vertical lines of a different length appear between his eyebrows, two irregular wavy grooves. I moisten my finger to rub them out, waiting for him to remark on my spittle. But he doesn't.

My imagination blossoms, produces exotic creations, songs which I dedicate to my lover. My singing voice is bearable, Carter says, and most of all he likes the lyrics to a song in which a delta and a river play the major role.

Since Carter never talks much about himself I remember everything he says. In this way he is not like me at all. He doesn't carry a diary in his head, always prepared to read from it to anyone willing to listen and expect to be praised.

'How things have changed. Have you noticed, Carter?'

Certainly he has noticed, but it is always me who mentions fluctuations, who displays knowledge and nudges and pushes the opportunities.

'Let's go for a walk.' I feel like running and demonstrating to everyone that I am in love. I catch reflections of my face that shines like the sun in the early morning. Carter is earth.

'Follow my trail.' But when he opens his arms I dance back to him. It's the trees that are dancing and the fountain.

'What exertion. Do you intend to learn to fly?!' he calls out.

I rip the words from his mouth with a swing of my arm.

'Tilly, behave, people are looking at us.'

I have to make giant steps to keep up with him. Carter points at buildings, the old and new, as they come nowadays. I have never seen them before.

'Have you seen this one?' I ask.

'No.'

'And this?'

'No.'

'Is this the city we have lived in for so many years?'

'It is.'

'It seems like a different city.'

Can you see me, mother dear? Now that I'm loved the world is in order. You approve of this union, don't you? You wouldn't say to me, No, Tilly, don't do it, would you?

I ask Carter about his profession. 'I am a computer designer,' he says, and I learn about computer generations, that we encounter the third and that one generation has a duration of seven years.

'If you had the choice again is that what you would choose?'

'Yes.'

'Why did you say that I remind you of Nefertiti?'

'I don't know. You do, that's all.'

'It's nonsense, but nice. I am Tilly and I don't know what that means.'

'One day you'll know,' he assures me.

'Now that I've found you it doesn't bother me much.'

He takes me by the hand and leads me to the bedroom. A bed rises from the floorboards that makes me whistle softly with admiration, a bed that was made in honour of Morpheus and love-making, a king-size bed, proud, ancient, carved, womb-like, riddled with history and the groans and mumbles of lust and enjoyment. Soon – any minute now – our combined sounds will sink into the veins of these venerable boards, and our tenderness will seep from the florid carvings.

Carter is long and lean. Bones stick out everywhere. His back is a copy of the map of astronomy, sprinkled with uncountable little stars and some big ones. I point them out to him.

'Who would have thought that freckles are stars,' he says.

'Carter.'

'Yes?'

'I just wanted to say your name.'

We tell each other how wonderful we are, how kind, bright, generous and understanding. And it is true. I cry, water of happiness. I rub my cheeks and say it is silly; Carter says it's all right.

The last cover drops. Skin shines with embarrassment. Choke on words. Lose them. Testing the air for approval. Stretching out arms to bridge the insecure moment. Holding and trusting. Walking a new path together.

Tower juts out of him, lonely and waiting, like a lighthouse. It nods at me and if I don't look at it for a while it collapses again, neglected.

'Funny tower.' Carter laughs, spurting it out like a rivulet.

I am bold now. 'I want your tower. I want to hide it. Make it rise again.'

'You make it rise.'

'Rise, tower!'

It jerks with effort to stand straight. Poor blind and naked thing, and so responsive.

Carter is much taller than I am, but his body fits nicely and precisely on mine, like his thumb into the palm of my hand.

'You first,' he says.

'Oh yes? What?'

'I'll wait for you.'

'Oh yes? Ah, that's good of you.'

His hands are good, his eyes and his heart. That is the best I can say.

'You are happiness incarnate.' Love is so pompous.

Carter doesn't answer. Doesn't he like being adored? Though it doesn't make any difference, because I'm a well of words.

'David must feel like you. Perhaps even God.'

'Tilly,' he says, embarrassed. When the flutters subside, he lowers himself. Alternately he kisses his two little rosebuds. Two times, four times, God only knows how many times.

THE WOMAN

We live in Golden Grove in Dorna Lane, number fifteen. Golden Grove is only a few miles away from the old city. We decided to move here when we got married. We figured that the way of life out here would suit us, a place for people who have their whole future ahead of them.

Golden Grove is one of the twentieth century's necessary inventions, a satellite city. Between the two ten kilometre sections of luscious fields and groves stretch the river and a highway. The more or less natural division leads us to believe that we stand as a unity. The name Golden Grove is well chosen.

Golden Grove spreads out comfortably, clean and prim. The overall impression is one of simplicity. Uniformity has been kept to a minimum by varying the style and height of the buildings, although with erections of that size variation has to be dramatic to achieve effect. Public buildings, two shopping centres, a marketplace and recreational facilities are scattered through the town. The streets are comfortably wide. The occasional group of townhouses make a pleasant change, but you cannot deny that it is a place where everything has been submitted to geometry. There are no lover's lanes, no funny old houses, no mazes or surprise views.

'It is perfect,' said Carter, who is infatuated with perfection. To him perfection is the epitome of thorough planning and mastery. He likes Golden Grove because it is the largest satellite near and far, it is quiet and has a few features the others don't have.

My wish is to live on the top floor one day, half way up to the sky, higher than most birds, but we have to start from the bottom.

When we planned the furniture, it was my wish to have orange upholstery and a fleet of cushions in the lounge-room. Not that orange is my favourite colour, but I saw some upholstery in burnt orange which caught my eye. Carter didn't object. He left the choice to me.

At first I saw a lightness when I looked at Golden Grove, created by the generous lawns. A few trees had been planted randomly, no more than five on each lawn, still in their nursery stage. Between the tall buildings they look as if they will never make it to a stately height.

From our lounge-room window I can see two trees, and with patience I can even see the grass grow day by day. Through the white custom-made curtains I observe people when they enter their houses. The contrast between house and person is emphasized by distance, and I can't help comparing the smallness of the people and the tallness of their achievements.

The view is similar from every window in town.

One faces a silent picture, like a gallery painting that draws the attention to details. On a clear day the houses are frozen against the sky. On cloudy days, when the eyes are tempted to wander with the clouds, the top floors move oddly against a natural direction, one of the visual tricks of nature.

The underlying geometry of the city *is* perfect. A perfection that is painless. A painlessness that evokes a longing. The longing seems quite unfounded, and I can easily detach myself from it but never rid myself of it completely.

Living most of my life in the maze of the old city I don't know yet whether I like it or not. It is a slow process. No wonder. We are used to the tumble. This town seems to be empty apart from the gatherings at the public places. Cars standing at the side of the road assume the air of neglected toys; their importance has faded.

At home I am often drawn to the window and there I follow every moving object outside until it disappears. It is strange in a way. You expect haste, but there is none, and the effect is intrinsic, like the taste of food without salt, or the galaxy without stars.

Sporadically old feelings of agitation come back, and I pace up and down and run outside as if to mingle with the crowd. Where is everyone? These buildings are towers of silence.

Living can be such a gentle affair that the present diminishes. I think of the past, but my past seems decades away and its pattern ancient. The only link from past to present is our wedding photo that smiles at us from the console.

It is the future I am really concerned about. To bear

children will be my purpose and the content of my life. This, of course, came about with Carter's consent. We haven't set a limit to the number of children. The reason for wanting them is that it is natural.

• 25 •

'While I wait for the child I will make a carpet,' I said to Carter. 'It's imaginative work, and it suits me. Besides, my hands are there for working.' Immediately I thought of my mother to whom childbirth had been so different, hard and cruel.

You've changed. Carter interrupted my recollections. 'I don't mean just the shape of your body, but your mind. Your face has a whole new expression – and there is something else, but words fail me.'

'I feel like a house,' I answered. 'My womb is a house. Yes, if you think about it – women are houses. We spend most of our life in a house, and a woman is the first house you live in.'

'It comes naturally to you,' Carter said.

'Women want children,' I said. 'What do men want? What are their priorities?'

'Men want to outdo themselves. Nature gave women childbearing and genius to some men.'

On the surface Golden Grove is a free and lenient place, but I feel as if I'm tied to it, as if I will never leave it. These days I often think of Florence, but because I've never travelled much it seems so out of reach.

Sometimes I get out my old books to indulge in the visions of Michelangelo's immortal men. They have lost none of their magic. But my own moves and footsteps in Florence are lost.

Carter remembers differently. He excavates the details of our journey. 'You were very much in love with Florence,' he laughs. 'You were always glowing with excitement. You curtsied before David and had your own idea about the sacredness of the domes and cathedrals. Remember when you refused to cover up your naked arms at the entrance? "My arms are not sinful," you said to the stern-looking watchman. You slipped past him and he chased after you and pulled you back, remember? Since then you've changed. Even your arms feel different. And you've become rather conservative in your outlook.'

'I've decided on my purpose,' I said, 'and that makes me feel purposeful. I don't know yet if I feel like a mother, but I certainly feel like a childbearer.'

'And what does a childbearer feel like?' he asked.

'Somehow I feel detached from ordinary things, even from myself, but in a subtle way. I feel a sense of limitation and I feel heavy, not just physically. My importance has come to the fore.'

'Yes,' he said. 'I see what you mean, and I'm a bit jealous.'

'Don't be,' I said. 'I'll share everything with you.'

I gave much thought to the carpet before I started on it, thinking it suitable for me in this condition.

'It looks good,' Carter said every time I showed it to him, and his hand stroked the carpet. Then he stroked my hair and the growing globe with the child inside whose arms and legs and fists grew stronger every day.

When the carpet was heavy and began to slip off my knees because of my advancing pregnancy I rested for a while and looked out of the window. An involuntary sigh escaped me.

Golden Grove is an island of tranquility. I daresay there is no town as quiet as ours. It astonishes me. A little. It troubles me. Sometimes. A little. Golden Grove is not famous for anything, no serious crime has ever been reported here, there is no smog, no disasters.

'It is perfect,' I say aloud to myself and take in the view.

The only time it is not quiet is when the man comes to mow the lawn. He is only employed to mow the lawns. Eight hours a day he walks up and down with his machine at some end of Golden Grove, an unpretentious figure in a blue denim suit.

One day a button was missing. It annoyed me greatly. I clung to it, made a big thing out of it. Perhaps he's not married, I thought, perhaps he's untidy, or married and both of them are slovenly. What is appearance and perfection to him? What moves through his head while he walks up and down? I bet all he thinks about is his grass all day long, with little variation on the subject.

I felt like walking up to the lawn-mowing man and offering to sew on his button. How I have changed.

Later, when the child needs to be taken out for a walk, I will sit with her on the lawn. Perhaps he will stop for a minute, turn off the motor and talk to me.

I will say, 'You're a brave man to mow the lawn all day long. Do you like your work?'

He'll say, 'It's okay. I like the fresh air. Is that your first child?'

'Yes. Do you have any children?'

'Yeah. Four.'

But he wouldn't know much about them. He'd say they're a handful, and that he has to feed them and see to it that they're clad.

'I wish Golden Grove was on a slope,' I said to Carter. 'It would add some interest to the place.' I heard myself sighing again.

'But it isn't situated on a slope,' Carter said. 'Perhaps the choice of land was a mistake. As I always say, you can never obliterate mistakes.'

'It must be my condition that makes me restless,' I said. 'And then again it could be the quiet. I often hear myself sighing.'

'That's because you're so big and plump,' he said.

'I'm a cow,' I said. 'Don't laugh! I often picture myself as a cow, one who is talking and sighing. My brain's a wilderness. Is everyone's? Carter, is yours?'

'Yes,' he said.

'You don't give the impression that it is. You seem to be perfectly adaptable. And so orderly. Ah, why must I talk about it? It's so trite.'

'Go ahead,' he said, then looked at my stomach and smiled. 'But I can't put my head in your lap to listen anymore.'

Because I was restless and full of nervous energy, the carpet was finished before the child arrived. I chose white as a background colour, the motif a still life with fruit in a pile. The design is straightforward, the colours appealing.

'I'll do better next time,' I responded to Carter's praise. 'I'll realize my own ideas, not follow any patterns, and I'll try out different techniques.'

The day came when my first child was born. I

commanded myself to be brave and humble. I felt like a vessel of clay that is about to break. In spite of a change of priorities that day, I made a mental note of the weather and a few details about the day including the important world news. Later, when she was old enough to take an interest in it, I would report back to her what I had observed on the day she was born.

I gave birth to a daughter with golden eyes and golden hair. No, not yellow. When a bright light falls on her, her hair shimmers golden.

'Tilly,' Carter said with a creamy voice when they let him see me. To release the pain he had suffered with me he pressed my hand so hard I gasped.

'It's all right,' I said, to convince him of our well-being.

Every so often I touched my surprisingly flat abdomen and ogled with vanity, which made me want to start flirting again.

Tension left Carter. His eyes filled with love. They had come in with the child.

'Here she is,' he said.

We looked down on her with pride. She was ours, to love and to care for. For one moment no mystery was involved in her creation. It seemed as if our intention and the act of copulation was all it needed to bring forth another human being.

• 26 •

I love to wrap her hair around my finger. It has the finest texture, and you want to fondle and play with it. When she talks with her hands, eager to unbosom me, I say, 'I can't understand you, my little one, I have forgotten the language of tiny babies.'

She smiles the smile of purest trust.

'Sure you can trust me,' I say.

To play with her, I get out silver and golden things and let them dangle in front of her eyes. All that shimmers has in it the shine of the sun and the stars. I remember it well, the magic that can be explained as a combination of light, colour and glass or metal.

Together we sometimes look into a mirror, playing friendly games with our likeness. When she cries so wretchedly that it could soften a stone, I say, 'It could be your belly that aches, or it could be that a great green monster frightens you. Don't be afraid, my little one, I will keep them at bay. Go away, monster, go away pain. While you must learn to speak, I must learn patience.'

This is so. And it is true that I won't be able to speak on her behalf. Slowly, imperceptibly, we will grow apart. All I can do is hope that we will not lose each other through misunderstanding. In years to come, I will not see her as she will see herself, and she will not see me as I see myself.

I am aware that bringing up children has its disadvantages for a woman. For many years to come, I will have to relate to an infantile world. It is a set-back where my own development is concerned. By giving birth, I have entered a new phase.

I have grown into adulthood.

At this stage, there are still other things besides the child. There is Golden Grove, and there are other people.

The first person I met when I took the child out for her first stroll around the block was Mr Wandel. He stood in front of the house. As soon as he heard steps he turned to see who it was. I noticed the odd thing about him first. His trouser legs flapped happily in the wind revealing his matchstick legs and pointed knees.

'Good morning,' he said. 'Have you just moved in?' He didn't pause between the greeting and the question. I looked at him with surprise.

'No. We moved in a year ago. But I haven't seen you before.'

'I'm new here. I'm Alderman Wandel.'

I introduced myself too, and we shook hands. Afterwards I looked at my hand as if it had been wounded.

'Very windy today.' I kept the conversation going, trying to avoid looking at him as if he were some kind of curiosity.

He didn't answer. His mind was on greater things. Mr Wandel, short and insignificant to look at, was full of surprises. Nature had made up for his physical shortcomings, endowing him with a voluminous voice, an instrument like a bell. He would have been a success on radio, and I assumed that he was successful as an alderman.

'I should have said I'm a journalist. I write a column for the *Morning Star*. Occasionally you'll find a contribution in Modern Living. My major interest is in architecture.'

'An interesting subject,' I said politely.

'So is town planning. I'd like to get into town planning.'

'I'd like to discuss Golden Grove with you. I'm interested in the place and its people.'

'And I'd be glad to discuss it with you.' He threw his hand and looked across the lawn. 'It's deplorable, there's no bench where you can sit down.'

'Couldn't you organize that as you're on the council?'

'I'll see what I can do.'

'It's a necessity rather than a luxury,' I said. 'I have a vested interest in having benches. When my daughter Ella grows up, I'd like to sit on a bench with her when I take her out. In autumn and early spring it's too cold to sit on the lawn. Is there anything I can do to get the benches?'

'Writing letters is a good idea. You'll get somewhere if you persist. I think that possibly we are disadvantaged here in Golden Grove. We can't count on further improvements.'

'Golden Grove is an island of peace and quiet,' I said. I could see these words framed, hanging in every entrance hall.

'Yes, that's the first thing that strikes you about the place,' he nodded and looked at our house, bending his head back far. Standing close to it there was no end to its height.

The child started crying. I looked at Mr Wandel who suddenly was as deaf as a stone. He shaded his eyes observing the next building. I bent down to talk to Ella. She stopped when I began to push the pram. Mr Wandel stayed behind. We are separated by a baby and her needs, I thought, and I walked fast until my fit of trouble passed.

Mr Wandel often lumbered in front of the house, his hands linked at the back, his thumbs agitated, looking deeply concerned. Unlike anyone else he became a well-known figure in our house.

Usually I reported our conversation to Carter who was not keen on making his acquaintance and had been lucky not to run into him. 'He sounds like a preacher,' he said.

'What's the matter with that?' I said, 'if he preaches something interesting.'

'I don't like people who preach.'

Mr Wandel, like a witch, drew people into his net most subtly. His victims listened patiently and were allowed to put in a word now and then. It was used to spawn a new idea. His idea. They couldn't win. Those who grunted at him and walked past him he dismissed as if they were air.

I didn't particularly like him, but I found him interesting. When I talked to him I kept my distance, to ward off the stale smell of body odour. His neglect of hygiene was his most overt flaw. I wished I had the audacity to tell him.

I wrote a letter to the council about the benches. I was determined that we should have them, and I also reminded Mr Wandel to use his influence. He promised to do what was in his power and suggested I get a petition together.

A few weeks passed. Carter began to suspect that I was Mr Wandel's most ardent follower.

I laughed, repelling his mockery. 'You don't know him. He has no appeal to me apart from what he can do.'

Others had mocked Mr Wandel in front of me for his idle talk; now I was doing the same. It was only a mild form of betrayal, but it stung my conscience. I changed my mind about talking to Carter about Mr

Wandel.

'I'm pretty sure that we'll get the benches,' Mr Wandel said when he saw me again.

'Oh good,' I replied and continued walking.

'I'm pleased too.' Realizing that I wouldn't stop as usual, he began to walk beside me. Not once did he look into the pram at the little round face. Sometimes, like now, her eyes would cling to me in an earnest, thoughtful, knowing gaze. It wasn't the look of an infant. What could I say? They were Ella's eyes, but it wasn't her look. It was one of nature's mysteries.

Mr Wandel was in a talkative mood and gradually drew me in. He became enraptured with his own words, waving his arms in all directions. While we walked around the block he talked about the city of the future. I divided my attention between him and the child.

'It has not yet been recognized that architecture should use psychology as a tool to serve us well and successfully. We are spiritual and sensual beings. Churches provide for our spiritual needs. They are, so far, the only buildings based on psychological need. It doesn't mean that living quarters should be replicate miniature cathedrals. It means a shift of emphasis, the amalgamation of several elements.'

'You'd have to get away from the high-rise,' I said.

'Yes, and provide underground parking to bring back the uncluttered view. While high-rise is still going strong, architecture already takes an introverted look at itself. We only realized a hundred years ago that our soul has requirements that are vital. Psychiatry is a young profession.'

The baby raised her pink arms and began her sign language. She looked as if she were in good company. I leaned over and whispered a baby word.

He lowered his baritone voice. 'Welfare is a subject that has hardly been opened up. You can carry it further, into legislation.'

'I don't think so,' I said.

'I have a vision of a city that has exceptional laws. A test case, so to speak.' He had raised his voice to a tenor overtone.

I pushed on faster. Mr Wandel kept up with my speed, unaware of it.

'Are you talking about lawlessness?'

'About less stringent laws.'

'It won't do any good.' I zoomed around the corner. We were back in front of our house. Mr Wandel didn't notice. Without interruption I began the second lap.

'Most people don't agree with it,' he said. 'We probably have to consider other factors first. Schooling for instance. A new education system. This can include the schooling of mothers.'

'The schooling of mothers?' I cried out. 'The schooling of fathers more likely. I can teach you, Mr Wandel, if you're interested.'

'Teach me what?'

I stopped abruptly. He nearly fell over the pram, balancing himself by stretching out his arms like a skater. But he still ignored the very nature of the obstacle.

'Do you have any children, Mr Wandel?'

'No.'

'Are you married?' I was bold and coarse, ignoring

his sudden vulnerability.

'You are a theorist, Mr Wandel. If I were asked my honest opinion, if I had a chance to speak from the bottom of my heart and will the world into my ideas, you'd be speechless. But to be able to do that I'd have to be in the front seat. Do you think that I'm eligible?'

'Mr Wandel didn't answer. He continued to walk round the block with me until we were back in front of our house. He bowed in an old-fashioned way and went inside.

Don't bow to me in an old-fashioned way, I thought, and without a break went for another lap around the block.

Carter would hear about our conversation as soon as he came home. Above all I would tell him about Mr Wandel's attitude towards me, the childbearer, and towards the child. He'd said nothing, and that was just it.

• 27 •

Sometimes when I talk to Carter about my daily chores, which are mainly repetitive duties, I wonder whether I bore him. But who escapes banalities? The one advantage I have over employers is that I don't need to discipline myself in order to keep time schedules and follow orders. My freedom is precious to me, but it is an insular affair. My working place is my island. There I can do as I please but not leave for the mainland. Machines relieve my workload. I take them for granted. But when it comes to computers I am daunted.

'What is it all about, Carter? Is it elitist?'

'No, it can be learned.'

'Yes, I know, but it still mystifies me, though you probably ascribe it all to logic.'

While Carter's other interest is foreign politics my interests lie closer to home, and they are more than my interests, they are my concern. Involving myself in local matters enables me to form a clear picture of our environment. Like an architect or labourer I participate in a fundamental process.

Sometimes I seem to wait all day long for Carter to come home from work. I stand by the window or sit on the couch, numbed by my invisibility. Progress has stopped, and the will is paralysed. Only the mind ticks over regardless. What else is there? I ask myself.

Behind many of the windows out there women are dealing with their loneliness in a similar way. Our thoughts stem from the same pool. We think of our children as being our future and happiness.

The web of my brooding is broken when the key turns in the door. Carter! I rush towards him. I buzz around him like a bee and push his desire for peace and quiet, which all day long weighs me down, out of the way.

A day of stagnation is followed by a succession of hectic days. Not one single incident is recorded and stored in my memory bank. Until one night the moon comes out, hanging low in the sky, huge and the colour of milk. We switch off the light, and Carter holds the child up to show her the moon.

A few days later I let the voice of a bird into my memory. It pierces the air for a mile and has a vocabulary that could be translated into human words. I open the window, but the bird is gone.

A group of people has gathered on the street crowding around a person who seems to be their leader. When he points his finger at one of the houses they all turn their heads in the one direction. Like magic their heads follow the pointing finger. What he tells them seems to be utterly fascinating. Since I can't hear what is said my curiosity is aroused. What is fascinating about the five or ten-storey buildings of Golden Grove? To find out I leave the house and walk up to the group.

When the group leader sees me, fifteen or twenty pairs of eyes follow his gaze, clinging to me as if I'm a statue of renown, and I am reminded of David in Florence.

The group's interest has shifted from my face to my middle part, and it is obvious from my condition what their thoughts are. Once that is established they take another look and openly reflect on me under the group's protection. They stick their heads together and whisper, and I catch single words like 'strange' and 'reminds me'. Will there never be an end to the guessing game?

The group leader makes an end to it. 'Where is the Remembrance Hall?'

'Twenty minutes walk from here,' I reply and put on a grim face, as if to say that they have trespassed. I dislike being singled out for my features.

'Is it open now?'

'Why shouldn't it be open? It's not a library or a theatre.'

He doesn't know what to say. He probably

wonders why I am so brusque.

I clear my throat and change my tone of voice. 'You can catch the bus over there.' I point to the far right. Thinking of the building in question I get chatty. 'It's a very interesting building, you shouldn't miss it. It isn't a church or a memorial for dead heroes. It's a place for everyone.' I interrupt myself. They should go and see for themselves, take a pamphlet that explains everything and buy some flowers to decorate the hall.

I adore the building, which has a really good atmosphere. At one end is an array of niches and steps you can sit on, and there people leave flowers and candles. Sometimes you can find fruit, a note or a card. Some people like to express their thoughts while sitting there and leave their notes for others to read.

The centre of the hall is an empty space, directly above which is a coloured leadlight. Sitting on the step you either focus on the leadlight or the empty middle, and you feel inclined to meditate. But even if you don't meditate you go away at peace. Occasionally the hall is used for recitals or plays.

The group is about to move on when I hear a loud whisper and afterwards an amused giggle. 'I wouldn't have thought it a good breeding ground.' And while they walk on I am rivetted to the spot. From that moment on I feel one with Golden Grove.

Golden Grove is not a place where you make friends, but then you find that it is less of a problem than in the city where you trip over people.

When we came here I saw some writing on a billboard. It said: 'Be friends with me.' I walked around smiling at people. Can you be my friend?

The group of people has moved away, and I stand there rather forlornly knowing nothing about them, why they came to Golden Grove.

Back inside I keep my eye on the window, but then I almost miss them. Dropping everything I run outside again. If I want to catch up I have to run. But I can't do that because I'm pregnant. I would look like an aeroplane that has trouble taking off. Standing in the middle of the street I watch their movements.

Soon they have reached the monument that stands where the highway meets the first street of Golden Grove called The Entrance. Of the four sides of the estate this is the closest to the old city. The monument that is planted there depicts two entwined 'Gs, the largest 'Gs to be seen anywhere in the world, I am sure, graciously curved from copper that has not yet corroded.

The group leader describes the 'Gs for about ten minutes while his people are bending this way and that, so that from the distance it looks as if he has asked them to do some exercises. What is he telling them, what is there to say about the entwined 'Gs?

They have probably introduced an extended bus tour from the old city, I say to myself, and walk away talking to myself until I enter the house.

When Carter comes home I tell him in detail about the group of people. He nods.

'Who were they?'

'I don't know. They were gone before I could ask.'

'Like people from another world, eh?'

'Yes, since you mention it. From another world. They made me accept Golden Grove for what it is.'

My new carpet is yellow with earth brown lions on it. They turned out to be handsome beasts, almost true to life. It is hard to capture them in handcraft, but I made a lucky choice of colour. Dominating the foreground the lions sit upright on their hind legs gazing the way lions do, as if what is in front of them is transparent.

When Carter saw it hanging on the wall, he turned and looked bewildered as if he expected someone to be standing behind him. Then he shook his head, amazed to have fallen for the stare of a creature that wasn't even real. 'Why lions?' he asked.

Carter would ask for a reason. But there was none. I had just followed a hunch. The lions were there, and that was it.

Apart from the male's imposing mane, the eyes are their most attractive feature. What I had in mind when I designed them were imprisoned lions, the only ones I have ever seen. But then I put them back into their natural environment. It was nothing like a humanitarian act.

Much time is spent making a carpet, so when the work is completed it tells about you. What does the design tell about me?

Soon my next child will be due. I must stock up on pickles. They go fast. Oh I feel heavy, weighed down like a tree in a storm. I moan and groan to Carter who looks at me with incomprehension. But he is well adjusted, he knows the secret of balance. He takes my hand like a priest who believes in the mercy of nature and a happy ending.

My second child is a son. His name is Felix, after
Carter's father who is an old man living in the
country. But I don't call him Felix. I call him
Methuselam. Felix is a name for the young.

'Here is one for me,' Carter says. He takes him and
holds him in his arm, and his son, in reply, starts to
howl. Carter's fondling hand drops as if he has
touched stinging nettles, and he looks at me
questioningly.

I laugh out loud, and Carter's hand comes back
with more confidence. He holds out his index finger.

'Are you one for me?' he asks and is delighted
when the tiny hand grabs hold of his finger and goes
back to sleep with it.

Our daughter when she sees her brother takes
refuge in her thumb and drives her head into my lap.

When Carter and the child are gone and friends
and neighbours are dismissed, I give myself to the
restoring powers that soothe and sedate and mobi-
lize strength. My body is free again from the extra
load and from pain. I look into the light that comes
through the window. Today is another beginning, for
me and my son.

I close my eyes and drift through the years I have
spent and will spend. One day when I am old and
the children have left me I might tend flowers or
dogs, and I might behave and talk to them as if they
were children. I might regress into simplicity, I might
think of flowers as children and of children as
flowers, and finally beginning and end might merge
into one.

Such thoughts I have sometimes. At my age! When my skin is still like peaches and cream and life is a succession of adventure and seduction.

The day arrives when I can go home. We have the opportunity to move to the third floor. From there we can view three trees on a lawn because we have changed from the north side to the west side. On every lawn stands a different number of trees, but never more than five. The three trees are closer to the house than the two we had before. They are silver ash trees, growing fast and looking beautiful.

Almost every day I take the children out for a walk. They play in the grass where they hunt the insects. There is not a great variety of them in Golden Grove according to my observation, and not one butterfly has come this way.

The lawn, of equal importance for the ecology and landscaping, is faultless. No weed, no clover has ever been able to settle and spread. The diligent lawn-mowing man paces the lawn in rain and shine – except when the rain is fierce – with his eyes on the ground, spotting every intruder, killing each with a small knife that he handles ruthlessly, like a professional slaughterman who never gives a thought to the poor helpless animal, deaf to its shrieks of fright. The man is taken by his knife. You can see it by the way he tries it with his thumb. His lips close tight and his nostrils flare.

He never wears anything but a two-piece denim suit, always in tip-top condition. Stoically he walks up and down pushing his thunder machine. If we are around he doesn't take any notice. We usually amuse ourselves with some toys, or pursue some ants or beetles in their track. If I remember I bring a magnifying glass, a device that reveals wondrous things to little Ella. To the lawn-mower man, we are not half as important as the lawn he has grown to perfection.

I must not judge him so harshly. His grim facial expression might be caused by a physical illness. Despite his ignorance of our inviting smiles, I decide to dedicate my next carpet to him.

To make up the lawn I will use a luminescent green. The lawn-mower man will be in the centre pushing the machine. White painted garden furniture will stand on one side. Tulips and daffodils will fringe the lawn. Butterflies will dance in the air.

The picture is clear in my mind. But there is something I haven't mentioned. I can see a large box, rectangular, lined with sky blue velvet. Someone is lying inside with his eyes closed and hands folded. The man is not sleeping. He is dead. The sun is shining on his face.

A coffin in my picture? And a white one. Why?

Someone else is coming into the picture. Two youths on roller skates chasing each other round the lawn.

But what is a white coffin doing in my picture? I can't erase it. The shadow of death is like the exquisite shadow of a tree. Golden Grove will look pretty, lively and gay on my carpet, shining with colour and movement. Despite the coffin.

It is late summer. To take advantage of the good weather I sprawled on the lawn today and started singing when I saw Vella come over with her six-year-old daughter.

I rolled over on my back but didn't stop singing. Vella sat down and joined in. We smiled at each other. I closed and opened my eyes and felt euphoric. My mind went back in time. I resurrected the child that ran uphill and fell to the ground and sank her face into violets. When the song was over, Vella leaned across and kissed my forehead.

'That was nice,' she said, 'You look a picture, and very happy.'

• 29 •

In autumn I met a woman standing at the entrance to our house, as if someone had dropped her off, told her not to move and then left her. Wisps of hair hung around her face, and her mouth began to pucker when she saw me.

I stopped and pretended to search for something in my bag while glancing back at her. She made big eyes like a child. I could see that she was lost and deeper in her eyes I recognized the scarred impression that life had made.

She, on the other hand, saw me as strong and superior. My smile lit a spark in her eyes, but she held back and waited for me to speak first. She was frail, her back bent, weaknesses wearing down first her handsomeness, then her dignity.

I don't want to be old, I thought spontaneously, it's too ugly.

'Yes?' I said, drawing the word out to prepare a path for her to talk to me unabashed. She had put her hands up to her chest where they dropped, resembling a dog on its hind legs.

I'm not going to be like her, I thought, not like a docile dog.

'Can I help you at all?'

'I am lost,' she said and waited anxiously for my reaction, hoping it wouldn't be hostile.

'Not lost,' I said lightly. 'You probably went in the wrong direction. That can happen to anyone, particularly when the streets and houses look much the same. Would you like to come in for a cup of coffee?'

'Thank you, yes, thank you, you are very kind,' she said, tilting into a sort of curtsy.

Up in the flat she busied herself with the children, making friends with them. Stroking and touching them she said, 'Two little angels, two soft little creatures. So adorable. And you,' she turned to me, 'you are going to have another one. Another little angel.'

When I asked her if she would like a drink she said she would like a brandy. As soon as I put the glass in front of her she picked it up, took a big mouthful, coughed, opened her mouth to cool it and made a sound when it hit her stomach. Soon she became talkative and free of inhibition.

'I walked for hours.' she groaned, 'I walked and didn't notice where I was going. My sense of time isn't very good anymore.' She giggled.'At my age time just passes as it pleases. Except that sometimes it stops. Then,' she paused for a time and with a sigh said 'you suffer. That's why I like to walk. It keeps the troubles away. They have no feet to follow you, they wait for you in your room or your bed.' She suddenly stiffened and poked out her head. 'Where am I? What is this place called?'

'You're in Golden Grove.'

'I haven't heard of it.'

'Golden Grove hasn't been on the map for very long. It's a few miles away from the old city. They call it a satellite town.

'That's interesting,' she said and took another mouthful of brandy. The need for coughing had subsided. She began to enjoy herself, nodding at me and the children, distributing smiles that furrowed her face in a pleasant way.

Her eyes were caught by my orange-coloured couch. 'Oh,' she said plaintively and began to stroke the couch. She had lost contact and sat as if she was by herself, becoming tearful.

'What is it?' I asked, watching her curiously.

'My Désiré, my poor Désiré,' she whined and began to rock from side to side. 'Her insides were strewn all over the road. The driver just drove on and the following drivers didn't take any notice. They flattened her brains. They were splattered everywhere. Pink splashes all over the road.'

'Who is Désiré?'

'My cat, my poor cat.' She shook her head vehemently.

'Do you only have a cat?'

'Yes, only a cat. Once I had children like yours. But as soon as they were grown up they left home. Now it seems as if they don't exist. They write seldom, and I haven't seen any of them for years.' She pulled a handkerchief out of the sleeve of her coat and dabbed her mouth with it. The coat looked like it was made from an army blanket, a sturdy piece, impenetrable to cold, and comfortable. It would outlast her.

'My children went to countries abroad, but not to
countries you would expect. This is a great century
for immigration. Once I thought that I could visit
them, but I could never save up enough for the trip. I
wrote to them to come and visit me, but they never
came. They married and when they had children
they were stuck completely. I became lonely quite
early in my life. My poor husband died twenty-one
years ago.' She dabbed her mouth with her handkerchief again. Ella, not used to the sounds of an old
woman, looked at her with great interest, her lower
lip pulled down by the thumb she had forgotten to
suck.

'Would you like another drink?'

'Yes, thank you.' And she held out the glass. 'I
don't drink usually, but I keep thinking of Désiré. I'm
sorry for crying. It must be the drink. Where did you
say I was?'

'In Golden Grove.'

'I saw two large entwined Gs on a pedestal.'

'That's our monument. I haven't made up my
mind yet if it's silly or significant, though I am sure
it's meant to be significant.'

'Désiré and I went for a walk every day.' Her
tongue began to trip over her words and I made her a
coffee, but her eyes were still glazed when she left. I
told her that the bus stop was next to the monument
and that she had to signal the driver.

I accompanied her to the front door and watched
her until she stood in front of the monument. She
walked around it and touched the lower loop and
bent in all directions. The heavy coat stood around

her like a tent.

I was about to go back inside the house when I noticed a few drops of blood at the spot where she had stood when I saw her first. I could trace the drops back into our apartment.

I went outside again. She was still there, circling the monument. As soon as I approached the exit, she began to walk away. I called out and waved, but she didn't hear me. Finally I caught up with her.

'You are ill,' I shouted, though I knew that she wasn't deaf. 'You are losing blood. Is it serious? Can I help?'

She jerked around so fast that my hand slipped off her shoulder.

'Sorry,' I said, 'I didn't mean to startle you.'

Her eyes wide, she seemed to fall to pieces, and I stretched out my hands to hold her. Faced with answering she weighed the truth against the lie. Her lips formed soundless words. One hand pulled at the big brown button, the other went in and out of the pocket.

Finally the truth won. She opened her coat, kind of tore it apart like a heavy curtain. From her hips down, fastened to her dress belt, dangled the squashed cat.

'Excuse me, love,' she said, 'Désiré doesn't look her best today. She is – she was – I don't want to lose her.'

• 30 •

He came into the world as Abel, the son of Tilly and Carter. Now I have one daughter two sons and three carpets. The children are healthy and I am content with my life and achievements. Although my old age seems to be light years away, I sometimes wonder. What it will be like when my ovaries cease to produce eggs? What it will be like when the children leave us? Maybe then I will change my mind about Golden Grove.

Already we live on the fifth floor. One day we will reach the top from where we will be able to overlook the whole estate, see its borders and beyond it. I am looking forward to it.

'Carter,' I said, 'We're on our way up.'

'Hmm,' he said inattentively.

'Yes,' I said, 'on our way up,' and I walked around the room with a growing sense of superiority. 'At this height you already feel you are raised above the common crowd.'

'Yes,' he said, 'time passes quickly.' His eyes were glued to some figures. He raised his hand and moved his fingers as if to link himself to what he'd said. Then he looked up. 'Since I've known you another computer generation has passed.'

'Oh, computers,' I said and quickly dropped my suspect tone of voice. 'Is it that long?' I remembered the day I asked him about his profession, I remembered the mood and the highly glossed colours. 'Do you still think about your old place above the river?'

'Your mind will always return to a place you have been before,' he said.

'Carter,' I pressed him. 'Look at me.'

He swivelled on his seat and faced me.

'Who am I?'

'Missis Wonderful.'

'Don't be silly,' I said, kissing his earlobe.

He kissed the tip of my nose. I kissed his Adam's apple. He put his hand on my thigh. I slipped my hand into his shirt.

'Oh,' he breathed. But his hand came between us pushing against me, to ward off my impetuosity. 'No, Tilly, no. I have very important work to do, Tilly. No, Tilly, no. Not now. Later.'

'Later is too late.' I snapped at him, threw my head back and sailed away.

I went to see Vella. She looked apathetic and blue with a cold.

'I'm not in an entertaining mood,' she barked against the music that spilled over from the room. But the door opened wide and I was sucked in.

Vella's slender back was ahead of me. She walked towards the record player and turned it down. But with the music down, my impulse to embrace her vanished.

'Turn it up a bit,' I said, and indulged in the light that came through the generous window.

Vella paddled back to the couch. Her drooping head stuck out of the blanket like a sickly blossom. She lived on the eighth floor in a building not far from ours. I liked to sit close to her window and look down and far ahead, and take the place of a helicopter pilot.

'You must bathe your eyes in light every day,' I said. 'You must open the window or stand outside and look at the sky. Doing that you will live longer and be more resistant to illness.'

Vella didn't answer. Momentarily she was absorbed by her virus that had gathered forces inside her, savaging the mucous membranes and passageways to the brain. Beethoven became ineffective. Helplessly her head rolled before the giant sneeze decided the battle. She lay slain.

The arm of the record player clicked and returned to start. I turned the record over.

'How is business?'

'I'm stagnating.' Her spirits began to revive. After using half a dozen hankies she reached for the Nivea cream, dabbing her sore nostrils with it. She looked like a child with the white dabs under her nose, and I felt motherly towards her.

'You're always stagnating.'

'I hate beautiful people. I would like to shave them bald instead of inventing new hairdos to flatter them. Their vanity repulses me. One day I'm going to sell the salon.'

'One day when?'

'I'd like to go to India, or Bolivia.'

'Alone or with Nadia?'

'I couldn't leave Nadia.'

'Where is Nadia now?'

'With my mother.'

Beethoven surged up again, widening the heart, filling it with grace and hope and illusions. I felt a thousand beautiful years old. I stared at the hair salon picture near the window without seeing it, until the massive wave of the music receded. Vella too lost Beethoven. She rose from her blanket nest and went to the cabinet. She poured a brandy. 'Do you want one?'

'No thank you, but I wouldn't mind a tea.'

We went into the kitchen. While she sipped her brandy I filled the kettle and turned on the gas.

The brandy turned her misery into sheer emotion. 'I love you,' she said.

'And I love you.'

A love call was her confession, solemn and luring. I sounded phony. Looking down, shame bending my neck, I saw Jackie, the turtle, slowly heaving his weight. Until the burning in my cheeks dissipated I tapped my fingers on the floor. 'Come here, Jackie, this way.' But Jackie was deaf from effort.

Vella could embarrass like a man. 'I'd like to hug you.'

I tapped away, expecting her to breathe down my neck.

'Don't say that, I don't like you saying that to me.'

If she wasn't careful she would kill my affection.

'Why not? Why don't you try? Have you ever tried in thought?'

'In thought you do a lot of things. It isn't valid.'

'Do you betray Carter in thought?'

'Yes and no. It's not me who does it in thought, so it's not real. I wouldn't betray him in reality.'

'That's fine. But kissing me is harmless.'

'So you've said before.'

'I assure you.'

The water boiled. I made tea. I imagined being kissed by her and was repulsed.

As if she was able to read my thoughts she said, 'I suppose in your imagination I take the place of a man. You're wrong. And it wouldn't be repulsive.'

I poured the tea. I tried to look at her objectively, the way I look at Carter sometimes, trying to understand him.

I couldn't see much of Vella now, and I couldn't

rely on my instinct either, because I didn't know her well enough. 'I don't like the sexual aspect.'

'I know. I'm not a seductress.'

'You're not?'

'No. I know you won't allow yourself to go too far.' She spoke casually. 'Maybe you'd prefer to be the initiator.'

'That's right, you're right. I think I'd prefer to be the initiator.'

Her glass was empty. Without thinking I extended my hand and laid it on her chest, watching her expression. I was pleased when she kept still.

'Say I love you again.'

'I love you.'

I shook my head withdrew my hand and looked at her thoughtfully. 'No one can say I love you like you do. You elicit the response you desire. You are a seductress.'

'Go home, girl.' She looked at Jackie who had stopped for a siesta only half a step from where I looked at him last time.

'I'm sorry,' I said to Vella. 'I would like to say something else, but I can't find the right words.'

'Don't worry. You do your best. Give my love to Carter.'

'Give your love or your regards?'

'My regards, since that is what you prefer me to say.'

'Do I hear resignation?'

'Yes.'

'I know that you mean give my love to Carter. They're your word. Not regards.'

'Is that what you hear? Go home, girl.'

When I came home Carter put his book down the minute I entered. He watched me walking up and down. 'Are you nervous? What's the matter?'

I established myself in front of him. 'There is nothing complicated about loving you,' I said. 'It's like lighting a match and lighting a candle with it.'

'Is that what it's like?' he said.

In the next room a brawl broke out. I went in to straighten it out. I didn't think of Vella for days after that.

• 31 •

Later in the evening I do the round, walking from one little bed to the next. There are four little beds now. No, three, to be correct. The new addition is a larger bed and soon another of the beds will have to be replaced.

I kiss my two sons and two daughters goodnight.

'Goodnight,' they sing and yell, a shifty mass of jelly under their covers.

About to leave the room I am stopped by a pink, frilled Ella who pops up and cries: 'Tell us a story,' and, taking for granted that I will, switches the light off in a flash. Snuggling into the cushion she fastens her eyes on the runner of light on the floor that leads out of the room.

'Quiet,' she orders the others.

Their giggling subsides. The last whisper makes way for expectation. Their eyes are set on me, the warder of castles and treasure chambers. I fetch a stool and place it away from the beds where the light from the other room fizzles out.

Baby Eva, paddling her arms in the air like a

puppet on strings, lets out a gurgle of joy.

'Tell us the story of the walking tree,' Felix says.

'Yeah, but first the one about the ant's cathedral,' Ella demands.

'And how the sugar became sweet,' says Abel and as usual adds, 'I like that story best of all. I like sugar.'

'We know that, silly,' Ella says condescendingly. 'Everyone likes sugar.'

After I have unravelled the old stories once more, the children roll up contentedly. They fold up like flowers in the dusk and fall asleep without delay. A sweet smell hangs in the air. No, not of baby soap. I am certain that it is the smell of their innocence.

Closing the door on them I am alone with Carter. I stare at him, but you can't dig Carter out of his journals by staring. I rub him here and there, softer here, firmer there, making myself indispensable.

'And how is my man today?'

'Fine,' he says, craning his neck for me not to miss another delectable spot.

'And how was your day? Good or bad? You, Carter, are you listening?'

'Good,' he says. 'It was good.'

'That's good,' I say. And after a while before his eyes slip back to the journal I say, 'Carter, I have asked you that for six years now and your answer is always the same. Always.'

'Yes,' he says. 'There's nothing else to say. Are you still happy?'

'Well,' I say, and pick a bunch of grapes from the plate. 'Well, since you ask, I am not deliriously happy, but I'm content.'

'I noticed,' he says, spreading his hands across the pages.

'Carter,' I say, squeezing some grapes into his mouth. 'I have to think up a new story to tell the children. Repetition dulls even the most exciting story. Have you got an idea?'

'How about a computer story? Once upon a time there was a computer who saw it as his duty to tell people never to tell a lie.'

'That's good. I'll embellish it.'

'Really? I'm glad to have contributed. Or tell them about love.'

'What sort of love?' I ask. 'I can't think of a suitable love story.'

'Some kind of love,' he says. 'There's a whole range.'

'Range,' I say after him, and it flicks the switch. 'Carter, you have inspired me,' I enthuse, pressing some more grapes between his teeth. 'I'll tell them about the bird who made love to all the flowers and animals in his kingdom, singing to them and pecking them gently, and when his family found out how far he went they accused him of being queer. The continuing accusations hurt him. Finally it wore down his defences. He developed all sorts of complaints, and in the end he lost his virility and his spirits turned sour. From then on he was a changed bird, a miserable little bird, no delight to anyone including himself.'

Carter laughs so heartily that tears roll from his eyes. How radiant he looks when he laughs. I gape at him as I gaped at David in Florence, and my heart beats madly for him.

To make him laugh and see him radiant I often become mischievous, or, as now, invent a story for him.

'Last week when I went to the old city I was standing near the dome when a man walked up to me and said, 'Would you walk into the dome with me?' My immediate response was to refuse, but think about it for a second. How can you refuse such a request?'

And so I spin my story, on and on. This particular one ends with sexual implications, but sometimes the thread breaks and the new thread knotted to the previous might be of a different colour. It doesn't matter. Carter listens attentively and smiles.

It is good to be a child now and then.

• 32 •

Not often but once in a while Golden Grove becomes the stage for some unexpected upheaval. Upheavals, of course, are entertaining, the ultimate form of entertainment, the participants acting out their true characters.

One day a noise that can only be likened to the crash of a broken window ripped the still air of our peaceful town. I jumped quickly to the window to investigate what the cause was and was faced with the spectacle of a dozen motor cyclists dressed in black leather and red helmets. They were riding around, making formations as if they were performing for a public. Tempted by the expanse of the lawn they soon left the roadway, and there on the lawn the performance continued. Very soon the grass was marked with the impressions of their wheels.

___

'Oh boy,' I said, thinking of our man in charge of the lawn.

The 1000 cc bikes looked like prehistoric insects imported from another planet, with pompous, abstract and unnecessary fixtures added, and exhaust pipes removed. I began to tremble at the sight and sound. But I was not impressed by them.

The formation outside began to dissolve and each of the black devils displayed his own spectacular act. They buzzed and whizzed about, encircling the houses, racing towards one another and just when you expected them to clash, they would dodge. I forgot I was in Golden Grove.

One of them with his legs spread wide apart finally rammed the corner of a house and fell off his vehicle. He lay on his back with his legs still apart, like a crab, the snorting monstrosity near his head.

'I hope you drop dead,' I shrieked, wondering if he would wring my neck if he heard me, and suspecting that he would.

The others stopped, parked their machines and walked over to him. They walked not too fast and not too slow but in the peculiar manner of seamen who had learned to distribute their weight broadly. But there was no ship and no sea under the stilts of this lot. Their ostentatious gait, the immobile posture of their shoulders were part of their showiness.

Their buddy lay flat on his back when they reached him. They observed him but didn't bend to help him back on his feet. Was he dead? Faces appeared in windows around, openly watching them. I, as usual, was not content to watch from a distance. A few minutes later I was at the spot of the accident. The man was still spread out on the ground when I arrived, booted and spurred, an obnoxious superman.

Bending over I met his eye. One eye was closed. But it wasn't bruised and there was no obvious reason for it to be closed, because in the open eye glinted a smile of amusement.

Amusement? I was not familiar with that kind of amusement. I didn't know what to do or say. He looked foolish, but with all his friends around him I'd probably lose out if I commented on his stupidity. I suspected that one of their rules was all for one and one for all.

They stayed on, thumbs hooked into belts or trouser pockets, legs apart, shoulders square, helmets askew as far as was possible. I kept a straight face although the vibrations I received posed a threat. They are like sharks, I thought.

Some blood dribbled from the forehead of the fallen bikie and began to dry above the brow. The blood held them in its grip like a Dracula movie.

'Blood,' they said. 'Blood,' lapping the word up, muttering and whispering it before they devoured it. It seemed to oil their guts and give them a boost and put them in the mood.

I, to whom losing blood is natural, felt they had a problem.

Suddenly the man's finger shot at me, restrained by the length of his arm. I jerked and jumped.

'Man oh man,' squealed the wounded bikie.

He cringed and laughed so hard he pounded the gravel with his fists. Eventually he scooped it up and strew it around, grabbed some more, stuffed his mouth with it and spat it out again. His other eye had opened as a matter of course.

I had no idea what was going on. Was he referring to my pregnant shape? Did it strike him as being funny? Was he trying to send me up? Or was he just uncontrollably silly?

One way or the other his laughter was contagious. It infected everyone but me. I stood like a pole. It was idiotic.

Not be be provoked I walked away. Their laughter followed me like a fire-spitting fuse. I began to run. In another minute I would dissolve with humiliation. My face was scarlet.

Suddenly their laughter stopped. I looked back to find they had withdrawn their attention from me. 'Thank God,' I said and was grateful that none of the leather-gloved paws pointed in my direction.

They stalked back to their bikes and mounted them. Man and bike became one, the bike thrusting from between their legs like a huge high-powered penis. Click-clack went the gears, and the gas sent them flying.

Standing in the doorway of our house I saw them leave. 'Joohoo,' they yelled when they saw me and revved up their motors. Fourteen times they circled the monument and left in a thunderous roar that hung in the air like the heavy shock of an explosion long after they had gone.

I could hear myself thinking again. Gently I pressed my abdomen, calmed my unborn child and checked our mail box. We had only one letter.

'We would like to inform you that there is a vacancy on the eighth floor in 12 Wilder Lane,' it said.

'Carter,' I said to him when he came home. 'From now on I will dedicate all my carpets to this town.'

'You've developed into a prolific carpet-maker,' he said. 'One day the town will be proud of you.'

'I see it as part of my purpose,' I said 'as it is your purpose to design, and our mutual purpose to make children.'

'To raise them more likely,' he said.

'Well, whatever. Okay then, raise them,' I complied.

Later in the evening I worked on my carpet, and while nimble fingers did wonders with stitches, my thoughts did their own weaving, continuously returning to the laughing bikie.

I took another look at my work. The design is difficult to describe. It is abstract, and I called it 'The Consequence of a Concurrent Decision'. The colours are purples, blues and reds. It is a genetic diaphragm fused by accidental elements.

• 33 •

'Christine,' Carter said.

Her name, feathery under his breath, descended on me from heavenly heights, hauling me up, out of my sea-like depth.

Now we have one golden-eyed golden-haired daughter, one golden-eyed brown-haired daughter, one blue-eyed brown-haired daughter, one golden-eyed golden-haired son and one blue-eyed brown haired son. They are all very healthy.

What more can one wish for? Do I complain about too much work? No. I say to myself, Look how rich you are. Yes, I am rich, and my wealth is a handsome lot.

Art came unexpectedly to Golden Grove, lifting the blinkers from our eyes. We didn't know where the work came from, but there seems little doubt that it was created by someone in town. One morning it stood on the lawn, a sculpture over six feet tall. It was made of bronze and steel, and it was the abstract figure of a man. Unconventionally he was turned upside down, and there was a square hole where the stomach should have been.

Everyone referred to the hole as 'the window'. The man's arms extended backwards like a swimmer who was about to make a leap in butterfly stroke. Small pieces of bronze were loosely fitted into wings and fastened to his legs. The metallic noise produced by the wind was pleasant, but the idea of flight was hopeless and probably meant to be. The head of the man was large and oval and dented all over.

It was not a revolutionary work of art, but recognizable shapes of the human figure would always find admirers.

I was hanging out of the window early in the morning doing some deep-breathing exercises when I discovered the statue. A car was standing at the side of the lawn. A man inside leaned his chin on his hand on the wheel, obviously contemplating the sculpture. He ignored the sign that said that parking was not allowed there.

Not many people would be interested in inspecting a work of art at that time of day, I thought, when a middle-aged woman with a red umbrella fluttered into view. Since there was no sign of sun or rain overhead, parading with an umbrella was sheer eccentricity.

The woman dashed forwards, stopped abruptly and composed herself. Then she walked around the statue with dancing steps, forwards and backwards again, using the twirling umbrella to placate her emotions. She looked rather dainty.

Swiftly I got dressed and went out to join the two spectators. The concept of the statue appealed to me. Not to miss a hump or groove, I touched it to trace the sensations its creator had sunk into it. The woman grimaced at me. For the time being I didn't want to be disturbed and ignored her response.

The bronze man was basically primitive. His intelligence was appropriately expressed with a technical attachment. His nose was enormous and massive shoulders hunched above a slighter chest. Instead of eyes he had eye holes. No attire was recognizable. Instead he was covered with small round pieces of iron.

The woman after me poked her finger in the eye holes, and then we looked through them. The indication seemed to be that we should try and see with the eyes of others. Poking was fun but like all fun it was over fast. I was left to think that it was childish.

'He's got the shape of an aeroplane,' the woman said with an affected voice. I had expected her to have that sort of voice.

'Hmm,' I grumbled and fumbled with the round pieces of steel that made up his attire.

The man in the car was still there. He glanced in our direction but seemed to have no desire to take a closer look. Was he the sculptor? I wished I had the courage to walk up to him and ask.

'I don't know why,' I said to the woman, 'but he reminds me of a bomb or a missile.'

'Is that good or bad?' she asked.

I shrugged but said, 'Bad.' I wasn't sure why.

'Why?' she wanted to know.

'Why? What is good about missiles?' I returned the question with another.

'Missiles are necessary to defend yourselves,' she said in a schoolgirlish way.

'Against whom?'

'Our enemies.'

'Who are they?'

'Don't you know?'

'No.'

'Well, we mightn't have any now, but we must be prepared for them.'

'It's all a bit far-fetched,' I said. 'Do you think the sculptor wants us to talk about missiles and enemies?'

She looked astonished. 'Probably not. What do you think?'

'Yes, why not?'

She didn't answer and followed her own thoughts for a while until she came up with a fresh aspect. 'I would have liked him to be half animal. Not necessarily Centaur or Unicorn. There must be other combinations. I don't know, I haven't got an artistic streak.'

'There will never be another Michelangelo,' I sighed.

'That's true. He was the greatest,' she said.

We were not the only ones who felt that the upside-down-man was controversial. That evening a large group gathered around, some children among them. Everyone poked and touched the statue and eventually a discussion began that split us into four. Some people wanted it to stay but not necessarily at that spot, some wanted it to be removed, some asked for a sculpture in which beauty and dignity could be recognized, some people approved of the statue without reservation. This group loved the statue because it was versatile, artful as well as entertaining. The 'window', the 'wings' and the 'looking glass' were suggested as suitable for games.

'Art has nothing to do with games,' some men rebuked them.

The children wanted to know why not? The men responded with impatience and condescension. It didn't take much to daunt the youngsters. The domineering adults didn't even notice when they gave up their place in the front row.

My friend Rose who had given them her vote followed them to the back row believing they needed to be comforted.

An unpleasant voice nearby diverted my attention. After all these years he finally opened his mouth. It was deplorable that the lawn-mower man had such an unpleasant instrument of communication. 'I don't want him on the lawn,' he said in an agitated high pitch.

When someone carelessly replied that the lawn was not the focal point, he blundered in again, 'I don't want him on the lawn.' He defended his case poorly and had no one to back him up.

The discussion went on. A man, tall and thin and bent over like a sunflower, with a strangely tapered forehead, came to a surprising conclusion on the subject of the statue's sex. 'Who says it's a man? Where is the proof?'

'It must be a man,' another man said. He was small and stout with a square face and bristly hair.

The egghead and the boxer exchanged duelling glances. The boxer gasped for air to reply and have his opinion sanctioned when a woman coyly said, 'It could be a religious figure. It could be meant to be Jesus.'

'Christ,' a man responded and with the sheer volume of his indignation crushed her out of existence.

'It doesn't matter what sex it is.' Another woman came in as a mediator, but then put her own case. 'I think he ought to go. Wings on legs! It's the utmost stupidity.'

'You have no imagination,' a man with a potbelly said.

'Yes I have,' the woman shouted. 'You look very pregnant.'

She won a few. But the cackle was sheer mockery to the rotund man.

'You're just jealous,' he groaned.

'Jealous?' she shrieked. 'Jealous?'

'Unimportant,' a new voice called out, claiming everyone's attention.

With an imperious gesture the man swept the two into silence as he would anyone else who would fail to see the 'Flying Dutchman' in the sculpture.

And so it went on until someone said we must

cultivate the arts and crafts in Golden Grove. Bravo to the artist who opened our eyes. If he is among us would he step forward.

But no one stepped forward. The group began to dissolve. As soon as I turned and approached Rose, the children vanished from under her arms.

'Let me carry the little one for a while,' she said and held her arms open.

I handed her over, glanced at the group of dissidents and said, 'Let's go. It's all over.'

While I walked ahead, Rose began to dance, following us. The little one croaked with delight.

'I love you, I love you, I love you,' Rose sang and didn't care about making a spectacle of herself.

The sculptor didn't come forward as many had hoped. Presumably he took a chance, and, intimidated by the voices against him, lost courage. Who could tell what sensitivities were at work?

Later in the week I spoke to Mr Wandel. 'The statue will be removed,' he said. 'It was decided today.' He spoke as an alderman, but then he expounded his view as a private person. He would have liked the statue to stay. I agreed with him.

The statue was removed two weeks later. Before it was loaded on a truck, I was able to do a few sketches of it. I didn't ask where they would take it. I didn't want to hang on to the real thing. And so my next carpet will be dedicated to the upside-down-man.

The lawn-mowing man walked up and down again with his face wrinkled in pleats of deep concern and anger that they had trampled down the soft green grass for which he had lost his voice. A week later no trace was left, the damaged grass had recovered.

• 34 •

No, I am not going to have another child. Something came up which made us reconsider. We decided to defer the decision about having another child. Maybe from now on I should devote my time to the five. I conceive like magic and children leave my body with ease, with stabs of rose-coloured pain, soon forgotten. Yes, I have been lucky not to suffer great pain when my hour arrived. Not like Vella who has only one child and doesn't want another.

Vella told me, 'I was in agony at the launching. It lasted two days and two nights. Mother Nature as a midwife was not what I thought she would be. She victimized me, cornered me, probed me again and again by inflicting pain on me I can only describe as torture. In between the attacks, when I was free of pain, I grappled with my anger. Why was I put through this endurance test? It is a launching cradle not a private organ, I said to myself. I suppose I solved the conflict to a lesser degree than others. On the surface what I resented most when I gave birth was my surrender.'

'I'm lucky,' I said 'that didn't happen to me.'

A few days after the sculpture was removed and after I found a note in the letter box announcing that there would be a TBC-examination unit coming soon, Carter came home with the news that he had an offer to go to an underdeveloped country for three months to hold a course on the latest development in computer design. He was his company's first

134

choice.

'What do you think?' he asked me.

'What do *you* think?' I returned the question.

'I don't like to refuse the offer,' he said.

'If you don't want to refuse the offer don't refuse it,' I said.

My answer pleased him.

'I am glad you are understanding,' he said.

'You're a computer designer,' I said. 'If you feel that it is important to you or that it might help the underdeveloped, then you must follow your hunches. I leave it to you to decide.'

'In that case I will accept the offer,' he said and stroked my cheek in case I needed to be consoled.

We talked about minor decisions and arrangements that would have to be postponed or cancelled.

'I'll write to you every day,' he promised, 'if I can.'

'Once a week if you can't,' I conceded. I was composed. Only my thoughts, usually occupied with everyday affairs and the children, went astray, went ahead like Carter's must have done.

I don't think that his decision was based on any other reason than that of interest in his work. It is not in his nature to be adventurous. He is a man of responsibility. But it must have pleased him to be chosen for the task.

The time of his departure drew closer. It was our first separation. Three months without each other would be a long time.

I heard myself saying, 'Carter, my love.'

'What's this I hear?' he said.

I was all over him. We looked back on our marriage. We had ceased to coo long ago. We had succumbed to a certain indifference, taking each other for granted. No, it was fine. I didn't want it to be different. If he had shown undue passion I would have laughed at him. Our bond was realistic now, with a high tolerance level. It suited me and it suited Carter. It was honest. Nothing could be so trenchant that it could separate us.

Ours was a union of luck. To do right by the other person was no great effort to us, and we still could smile effortlessly at each other.

The night before Carter left, I was mending. Carter sat opposite me on a two-seater studying his brochures. I dropped my mending and looked at him. Often he had been a shadowy presence. Now he was the only man in my life.

I took his hand and held it gently. He raised it to his cheek. We didn't speak. Our hands were finer instruments than our mouths. Sometimes Carter gazed into my eyes, and I kept myself open. We sat like two lovers on a riverbank watching the water flow by.

'Look after yourself,' I said at the terminal. 'And keep away from the war.'

'Yes, I will,' he said and smiled.

The country he went to was at war with its neighbour, but Carter wouldn't have anything to do with it. He would be training a group of men. His duties were outlined. The war was a black African affair.

His last kiss at the airport was a warm and strange seal. His lips were very close to me, his mind was far away.

The children and I went home and while they

played I sat between them, not paying attention for a long time. But what is a long time when there are whirlwind children around? They soon captured my attention with their simple tricks. Carter, I thought, while I spoke about something else. Next day my mind went traipsing into the grey zone that stretched between us.

Carter's letters came regularly once a week. At first he was very excited about his new environment and gave me a colourful description of it. Two letters later he began to focus on us and asked about the children and what the news was in Golden Grove.

There were a lot of things I could report on. I didn't want him to miss out on the happenings here and explained in detail about daily events. I told him about the new plan for a hot-house, that we were going to get an additional communal swimming pool, that Ella thought of him lovingly every night, and that I had begun to read the history of Alexander the Great.

Letter writing was a poor substitute. I missed him, and I believed that he missed me as much. The moment of receiving his letter was one of great exuberance. Taking the letter from the letterbox I would press it against me and run back inside as if I had wings. 'Dearest Tilly,' I would read, and 'Dearest Carter,' I would sing.

Two months passed and I began to look forward to his homecoming. Two weeks later he unexpectedly wrote that he couldn't come just yet. It was the longest letter he had ever written, and my reaction to it was one of horror.

Carter had involved himself beyond his duty. He

had put off talking about it to me and had managed to hide it successfully.

The country was small, the war and the famine were close, and Carter could not just board a plane after his work was finished. Golden Grove was at the other end of the ocean; it was obvious that he had lost touch.

Carter had never expressed himself negatively, but he had never known the true meaning of terror. This had momentarily changed. A disruptive way of thinking marked his letter and he struggled with a new vocabulary.

I cried and poured myself a large glass of gin to keep things in perspective.

It was not the destruction of war that was Carter's chief concern, but the children who suffered most. He talked about them as if they were his own.

As usual I turned on the television for the evening news. A few minutes were dedicated to the war and the famine in that far away country. After the news there was an exclusive report.

I had watched these reports before, but none of them, in spite of their visual explicitness, had the plasticity of Carter's letter, which had me genuinely involved.

Now I sat in my cushioned chair and listened to every word.

I watched the reports almost every day. The impact of the cruelties was exclusively reflected on my intellect and only as long as the picture was there before my eyes. I stored it like a school history. And though I had no audience I loudly deplored the warmongers.

When I turned off the television I saw no contradiction in telling tales to the children and reading educational stories to them. Golden Grove was a perfect place! It was our silken cocoon. Destruction would never come near us.

Alcohol and the truth eventually threw me off balance. I couldn't focus the room. I was mesmerized by the event and confused like Carter.

Carter, a placid man, had lost his poise. Would he be the same on his return? My foundation was shaken.

'I musn't let it get me down,' I said to myself. 'I must face up to it and be strong.'

• 35 •

I opened the letter with fearful fingers. 'My Dearest Tilly,' I read. My eyes slipped away out of the window to the rooftop of a house. Above it lingered a grey-tinted cloud and fate in unfathomable depth. I wished the letter would say, 'I will be home tomorrow.'

As if the words weighed heavily they dropped towards the letter's edge, revealing Carter's depression.

'The children,' I whispered under my breath, 'the children are everything. Forget the others. Think of yours. They are fine. Our children are fine. They have been taught to think that the world is a wonderful place.'

I continued reading. The sentences came unstuck before my eyes and I swallowed them like medicine. They entered my bloodstream and took command of my thinking, and though in a way my thoughts paralleled Carter's I became doubtful that I would follow him all the way in this.

My Dearest Tilly,

I haven't received your reply yet to my last letter in which I told you about this country's war, how I see it and how it affects me. I am tired, and I suspect I am not altogether in command of myself. Thoughts and feelings are jumbled together. I don't think I can blame it on the oppressive heat.

Coming home in the evening I have long showers. Afterwards I sit and relax with a brandy. I start my positive thinking by saying, 'I must go home at once,' but I stay put and stare in front of me, and the pictures passing through my mind are not of home. I am crowded by hundreds of small dust-coloured children many of whom will die tomorrow. I can never recall our children's voices, but what I hear is the whimpering of the starving. I have become a sounding-board of their plight.

The problem is huge. It can't be solved, and I am convinced that it will happen again somewhere else. We are not heading for times of peace and ever-lasting happiness.

Tilly, was it right for us to think that having children is a private affair between you and me? Must we not consider other aspects? I have become suspicious of our motivation. We didn't think at all of the sort of world we put our children into. I want our children to be happy and protected from evil. How can I protect them, how can I keep those forces that do damage away from them? I'm afraid it is not possible.

Dearest Tilly, because I feel responsible, I think of the children here as my children. The people who came here to help, working in the camp and the hospital, feel the same responsibility. They work hard to avoid thinking too much about the misery they deal with, and to keep frustration at bay. I can't imagine anyone who doesn't pray.

I am looking forward to your reply. It will help me to break the spell that has prevented me from coming home.

Love Carter

The letter fell to the floor. It was quiet, peaceful, tranquil. It was truly that. I was faced with two truths, but it was easier for me than for Carter. I could stave off the irrationality that came through to me from his letter. My reality was not distorted.

The children. It was a compulsive thought. To convince myself of the well-being of the smaller children I went to the kindergarten where they were supervised. The girls in charge were devoted. They wouldn't have thought of politics and war.

I squeezed the children and we laughed and joked, but underneath it I was disturbed. Everyone but I was rooted here. My thoughts went out to Carter's adopted children.

The attendant offered me a cup of coffee. One day I would talk to her about Carter's experience and his thoughts on having children. I crouched in front of some neglected toys, picking them up and putting them down. Children know instinctively how dead toys are. They never play with them for very long but soon learn the art of make-believe.

Carter, come back, I signalled. It is not for you to stand up to it. It is not your war, not your famine, not your responsibility. They are not your children.

Divorce yourself from it. Your world is here.

When later in the day I answered his letter, it seemed there were no right words. My concern was Carter, and I disregarded the plight of the others. The situation was complicated and beyond my understanding. I was afraid.

· 36 ·

Carter is back. His homecoming was not what I had hoped for. I had cautious words prepared, gentle smiles and embraces, a merry show. We had made a welcome sign and hung it up above the entrance door. Flowers and balloons were painted on it by the children.

We all went to the airport, and we watched the planes coming in. Finally Carter appeared. He was one of the last passengers from his plane to go through customs. Slowly he slouched toward us, thin and dark and hesitant. My heart missed a beat. The children leaped forward.

Carter was overpowered and possessed. They planted kisses where they would hit, on his nose, chin, mouth, hands, legs. They climbed on him like monkeys, hooting sounds of conquest, fighting for attention in a war of jealousy.

Through all the young heads I saw his eyes. Only the lines around them came out in a dutiful smile. His mind was not with the load of good luck in his arms, nudging and licking him with affection. His mind was with the children of tragedy.

We kissed above the wave of the children's limbs. 'Welcome,' I whispered, and between the carelessly bubbling lips I found his. The kiss had no message:

no joy, no longing.

'Hello,' he said in a tired voice.

The children crawled all over him.

'Your father is tired,' I said to them. 'Take it easy, will you?'

'I want to go on an aeroplane too,' Felix demanded.

'Last week we moved to the top floor of the building,' Ella shouted. 'Mother said we've been lucky to get the flat. I helped to move boxes and chairs.'

'That's very good of you,' Carter replied.

'There's a river in the distance. Do you know which river, Dad?' said Abel. 'I want a boat.'

'We'll see,' Carter answered.

'You always want things,' Ella scolded Abel. 'You're never satisfied.'

'Why shouldn't I want things?' he asked her.

Ella ignored him, turning from him to her father, rubbing her cheek against his arm.

'The river looks like a snake from the top floor,' she said. She held his hand with both her hands to stop any competition for it.

'I want to go to the zoo,' said Eva.

In that fashion Carter was welcomed back, and it seemed not much different from what it had always been.

Later we sat around the table for dinner.

'I cooked your favourite dish today,' I said. Holding a bowl of rice in my hand, I turned to see his face.

'Fine,' he said. His voice was impenetrable, as if he had geared himself to be patient.

I stopped, resentful. I hadn't thought. The children. Famine. Then I shook my head. I couldn't let it affect us all.

'Good,' I said defiantly.

'You look gloomy,' Ella said. 'You look as if you're unhappy to be back.'

'Don't say that,' I said to her.

'But he does look gloomy,' she said. 'He doesn't look cheerful, and he doesn't look as if he loves me. Do you still love me, Daddy?'

'Of course,' Carter said.

'It doesn't sound as if you do.' she said.

'Don't say that,' I said to her again, glancing at Carter. 'Your father loves you very much. Don't doubt that.'

'All right then.'

'I broke my train.' Abel crawed from the other end of the table. 'I need a new train.'

'Your father doesn't want to know about that now,' I said to him, feeling protective towards Carter.

'Don't you want to know about it, Dad?' he asked.

'Yes, I want to know about it,' Carter said patiently.

'See,' Abel said to me.

I looked at Carter to share with him the smile of amusement, but Carter was solemn and locked into his solemnity like a nut in a shell.

Patience, I said to myself and conquering my impatience, put my hands on his shoulders.

I remembered a landscape of harsh granite mountains on an overcast day. As we were driving along, the sun broke through the clouds and showered the rocks with golden light.

———

A change would also come to Carter, but it would be gradual. He would not return to the unlucky country. No sound, touch or smell of it had a hold on him now. Soon the memory of the war and the famine would fade. I was optimistic.

'It's time to go to bed,' I said.

The youthful commotion subsided. Mannerly Carter was kissed goodnight. One after the other they smacked a kiss on his cheek, and Carter pulled faces to make them believe that he was a funny man.

'You do look thin and gloomy,' Ella said again. 'I hope you recover soon from that flight.'

'That's enough for today,' I said to her. 'Put the others to bed, please.'

The house fell silent. I switched off the main lights and looked at Carter who held a magazine without reading it. I waited for him to speak. When I couldn't bear the silence any longer, I sat down on the carpet in front of him and took hold of his leg.

'Hello, there.'

'Hello.'

His mouth was unwilling now to pretend. He drew shadows and gave himself to them.

I ignored my observations. 'Carter,' I said cheerfully, 'you're back.'

'Yes, I am,' he said formally.

'With us again,' I said. 'Don't think back.' The subject couldn't be avoided.

'Not on purpose,' he said.

'Our children need you.'

'Five children,' he said.

'They're angels,' I said. 'At least to us they are. You always called them angels, remember?'

'I don't know.'

'You don't know? Of course you do.'

He didn't answer. He seemed to sink away and only the power of my voice seemed to pull him back.

'Yes, you do. They're angels. You're right. They're lovely children, and everything is all right. Listen, Carter, and look at me. Isn't it true that we got what we wanted? It took time and care and effort, but we made it to the top. I am glad, and most of all I am glad that you are back where you belong. Come down and stretch out next to me. That's it. All right now? Close your eyes and relax. Relax your eyes too. I can see them moving under the eyelids.'

'Here is your body, your arms and your legs. And there is your head. Empty it of all your scrambled thoughts. Get rid of everything. Don't leave one letter. Do you feel contentment rising? Try, Carter.

'Somewhere here is your tower. Yes? No tower? Must be. Wait. Give it to me now. Let it grow, into my hand, out of my hand, into me. Now you are here and nowhere else. Yes? Remember what I called you once?'

'Hmm.'

'You're a good man.'

'I doubt it. I am so – ' His hand lifted and dropped. He left the sentence unfinished.

'Don't doubt,' I said. 'You must not doubt.'

· 37 ·

Although Carter has been back for a few days, he remains sombre. It will take time, I keep telling myself; he will come out of it soon.

Yesterday he went to the old city to arrange his

146

return to work. When he came home, he had a newspaper under his arm. Later, when he left the room, I got rid of the section that had a picture of the war in it. To my relief the news was no longer a subject that was given priority. I was relieved.

'You haven't seen the view yet,' I say to him. 'Now's the time. We're all together. Why don't we go up to the rooftop for a while. The weather is perfect today. We should have a good view.'

He nods. I gather the children together.

'All set?' I lift Baby Christine, to carry her on my arm.

There are only two sets of stairs to the top. The children are running ahead straight to the parapet. Carter and I join them, and we walk around to get the full view. Beneath us spreads Golden Grove in its entirety, neat and clean. In the distance the river, a silvery snake, settles in the landscape. Soon the children begin to lose interest and turn to play.

'I must say I pushed to get to the top,' I say. 'They soon knew in the office. It helps to make yourself known. In the end they didn't ask me anymore what I wanted. They came to the desk and either said there is no vacancy or you can move up one floor.'

Laughter splutters forth. I join in with the children. We look at Carter invitingly, but he doesn't respond. It will take time, I keep telling myself. His profile is one quiet line. The descending sun show signs of exhaustion, a deeper yellow. Carter holds out his face to receive ablution. God bless you, Carter.

'Let's sit down, shall we?' I take his hand, and he leaves it to me, a limp cold thing. It touches me strangely and gives me a sense of being old. I squeeze his hand, harder than intended and, I lead him like an old man, to the table and chairs at the corner.

We sit down and watch the children dashing by, colourful arrows in their jumpers and dresses. I take in their sound and nod at Carter. Nod, Carter, nod back.

'Catch me,' they shout as if they were hard of hearing.

Little show-offs. Aren't they just lovable, Carter? He has merged with the back of the chair. He sinks my smile. His face is pale. His mouth opens. His hands on the armrest turn over, and his fingers open and close.

'Carter, love, are you not well?'

'Rattattattattatta.' The small boy's voice blasts into our ears. He is holding an imaginary gun.

Our daughter drops to the ground, pretending to be hit. He looks deeply satisfied and gives her an extra blast.

'Carter, love, are you not well?'

His fingers open and close. His mouth quivers. He can't speak.

'I'll get a blanket. Is that what you need?' I take his hand again. 'It's chilly.' I rub his fingers and blow them warm.

His eyes are blank.

'Carter, what is it? Please, say something.' I begin to shiver as well. I put down the little one and call Ella to watch her.

'I must go and get a blanket.' At the exit I turn around.

Carter has remained in the same position. Baby Christine sits at his feet. The others arrange themselves in a four-compartment train. They hiss and puff and whistle.

I hurry. On my way down, I try to figure out what I can do for Carter. A brandy might help him, yes, and later we will see. Maybe he needs a doctor.

I get out the blanket, fold it, and pour some brandy into a large glass. If nothing else it will get him out of himself. As I put the bottle down, I hear shrieking in the distance.

It is one of those days, I think, on my way to the door.

I open the door, hear the trample of footsteps. The next moment Ella appears at the bottom of the staircase and takes one long leap towards me, her arms extended.

She throws herself against me and stops me from moving. Her shrieks turn into convulsive sobs.

'Ella,' I say, 'but Ella. What is it darling?'

'Father,' she shrieks, sliding to the floor.

'Get up, child, we must rush. I know he's ill. I came down to get him a blanket and brandy.'

She shakes her head wildly, applying great strength to cling to me.

'No,' she winces.

'Come on, darling, get up. You must get up and tell me.' With effort I bend over to put the glass down away from us. Her face is demented with fear. 'Ella, sweetheart, don't be afraid. There's nothing to be afraid of. Let's go and see your father now.'

She gathers the full power of her voice. It echoes from the walls. 'No, he'll murder me. He murdered the others. He came after me. He's not my father anymore. He's a murderer. He'll kill me!'

'Child,' I say, focusing on the glass of brandy on the floor. 'That is not true. It is just not true.'

Her shrieks in my ears, I look at the stairs that lead to the rooftop.

Not long ago I thought that we had come to the top. Now I find that this isn't so. There will be more stairs to climb after this.

Also published by Penguin

BEACHMASTERS
Thea Astley

The central government in Trinitas can't control the outer island. But then neither can the British and French masters.

The natives of Kristi, supported and abetted by some of the *hapkas* and *colons* of two nationalities, make a grab for independence from the rest of their Pacific island group. On their tiny island, where blood and tradition are as mixed as loyalties and interests, their revolution is short-lived. Yet it swallows the lives of a number of inhabitants – from the old-time planters Salway and Duchard, to the opportunist Bonser, and the once mighty *yeremanu*, Tommy Narota himself.

Salway's grandson Gavi unwittingly gets caught up in Bonser's plans and, in a test of identity too risky for one so young, forfeits his own peace.

THE FLESHEATERS
David Ireland

A novelist who lives up a tree; a child who likes to paint dead bodies; a granny who lives in a kennel and bites ... these are some of the characters of this extraordinary novel set in the dilapidated stone mansion in Sydney. Bizarre, bitingly satirical, richly ambiguous, it is an image of the modern world which the author sees as a 'madhouse without walls'.

DIRTY FRIENDS
Morris Lurie

In Tangier a lonely poet confronts the ugliest
truth . . . in Greece a millionaire makes a
dazzling escape . . . in Yugoslavia a marriage
falters . . . in Melbourne a friendship shows its
other face. . .

Wherever he is (Switzerland, New York),
whomever he addresses (a fancy mistress, a
wry Jewish uncle), Morris Lurie displays that
uncanny mixture of humour and compassion
which has won him an international audience.

'Reading Morris Lurie's stories . . . is like having a brilliant, funny friend. It's not that he's
always good for a laugh, which he is, but also
that he's a help when the going gets tough. He
faces sadness, even tragedy with spirit.' Bruce
Grant, *Australian Book Review*

'Lurie has that kind of acute appreciation of
social farce that tots up to a real observation of
the styles of the culture.' Malcolm Bradbury,
Guardian

'a real feeling of civilised man's unease in an
urban environment where nobody seems to fit
. . . good serious entertainment.' R. G. C. Price,
Punch